Vicar Rhomes has had the honor of being head honor guard to King Leortis—the dragon king—for several centuries. Escorting the king to Savannah to discuss a rogue dragon they're tracking with the Shifter Council is normal procedure. Joining a couple of councilmen for a meal, Vicar fills his plate only to stumble over a pretty auburn-haired cutie . . . spilling his clam chowder all over the poor man. Mortified, Vicar snaps at the shifter. It's only after the blushing beauty strips his shirt that Vicar gets a clean whiff of his heady scent and learns who the man is to him—his mate.

Getting doused in clam chowder isn't the worst thing that's ever happened to Desmond while working in the cafeteria. It's the blistering put-down spouted by the huge, gorgeous black man that makes him blush. After whipping off his soiled shirt, Desmond assures the male that he'll get him a fresh bowl . . . and is shocked when the guy does a one-eighty—nearly falling all over himself to apologize. Then Desmond smells the man, and he realizes the source of his sudden change. The guy is his mate . . . and he's not just a dragon, but a powerful one. While Desmond wants his mate, he remains wary. He can't help but wonder which personality is the dragon's real one.

Can Vicar figure out how to continue to do his duty to his king while proving to Desmond that he's not an unmitigated jerk?

Stumbling Over His Love
Copyright © 2023 Charlie Richards
ISBN: 978-1-4874-3890-6
Cover art by Angela Waters

Published by eXtasy Books Inc

Look for us online at:
www.eXtasybooks.com

Stumbling Over His Love
Shifter's Regime 13

By

Charlie Richards

DEDICATION

First impressions are always unreliable.
~Franz Kafka

CHAPTER ONE

"Gaithnos has been stripped of his title as elder and has been labeled rogue," King Leortis Vermilion told Councilman Regales Colearian. The dragon king sighed as he shook his head. "I apologize it took nearly six months to make it happen." Leortis smiled ruefully. "I may be king, but I still have to deal with the damn diplomacy of placating the elder dragons."

"Diplomacy does suck sometimes." Regales winced before clearing his expression. A curious gleam entered the grizzly shifter's dark eyes. "How much power do the elder dragons really have? Are they elders like the gargoyles' Circle of Elders? Or is that just a title?"

Vicar Rhomes barely resisted allowing his eyes to widen in surprise at the blunt questions. The inner workings of dragon royalty and culture were a closely guarded secret. No royal dragon wanted to admit that, on occasion, their hands could be tied by a bunch of overbearing, aging dragons.

Sitting in the opulent lounge, with nearly a dozen people in the room, Vicar wondered how King Leortis would respond.

As head honor guard to King Leortis, Vicar had the duty and honor of escorting his king just about every time he left the palace. He'd been offered the post by Leortis when he took over as dragon king from his own sire over two hundred years before. Vicar took great pride in his duties.

To that end, Vicar stood behind and to the left of where

King Leortis sat in the large lounge. Besides Leortis and Regales, there were four other councilmen in the room. Guard Warzer—a fellow dragon who also acted as his driver—stood near the door behind them. There was also one shifter guard for each councilman present in the room.

Way too many people to be privy to dragon secrets.

"The dragon elders are any dragon who's over two thousand years old and wishes to sit in on certain meetings," King Leortis explained, surprising Vicar with his candid reply. "For the most part, dragons that age are solitary, so most don't bother." With a shrug, the king added, "And the only way they could overturn some edict I've passed is if they are unanimous."

Behind Vicar, Warzer bit back a snort.

Leortis smirked as he peered over his shoulder at the green dragon, who looked like a blond bruiser in human form.

When Leortis turned back around, Councilman Vincentius Goldstein arched a dark brow. "I'm guessing that doesn't happen very often," the lion shifter quipped.

"Uh, no," King Leortis confirmed. Letting out a soft chuckle of his own, he told them, "Dragons really are notorious for arguing just for the sake of it."

Vicar mentally winced.

Yeah, dragons can really be opinionated elitists.

"Anyway, if any of your people hear anything about Gaithnos's whereabouts, please pass it on to us as swiftly as possible," Leortis continued, returning to the original subject. "We've had a few leads, but so far, nothing has panned out."

"Absolutely. We'll get the word out and have our people keep their eyes open. It's about time our people have come together more," Councilman Lorian Bakerman agreed with a dip of his bearded chin. The buffalo shifter's deep brown eyes twinkled as he continued, "And speaking of coming together, let's move on to a much happier subject." With a grin, Lorian finished, "Charon's impending birth."

That was the second reason for King Leortis's trip to the outskirts of Savannah, Georgia.

Charon was a young omega dragon who'd recently found his fated mate in a Komodo dragon shifter—Dakota Drudeson. Due to former elder Gaithnos having a spell cast upon Charon, the pair had been in the vicinity of each other for years before they'd realized they were mates. Their exuberance at finally discovering each other had resulted in Charon getting knocked up first thing.

Fortunately, both men were looking forward to the addition to their family, and Dakota had two brothers who were mated and would be there by their sides to help.

With only one of the pair being a dragon, however, that left the small problem of hatching the egg. It required the flames—or ice—of two dragons to hatch it. That meant the pair needed help, and Charon had no acknowledged family.

"I'm truly honored to step in and assist Charon during this momentous occasion," Leortis stated with a grin. "I haven't taken part in a dragon birth in over a century. Not since my heir was born, Leonidas."

"And we've never seen it," Councilman Nigel Granis admitted with a wry smile. The tiger shifter relaxed in his seat, resting his left ankle on his right thigh. "It'll be an honor to be part of the ceremony."

Unable to help himself, Vicar blurted, "You're going?"

Nigel nodded, a smirk slowly curving his lips. "Since he started joining our barbeques, a number of us councilmen have gotten to know Charon." He waved his hand to indicate the other smiling and nodding men in the room. "Charon is a wonderful man." Leveling his gaze on Leortis, Nigel commented, "I understand you raised him as a ward. His parents left him with you?"

Leortis grimaced even as he nodded in confirmation.

"While omegas have been a part of our culture from the beginning, there are still a few narrow-minded dragons who think they're weak or unnatural." The king sighed heavily, sadness filling his countenance. "He was left at our gate as a toddler. From what I understand, Charon has very few memories of his sire." With a very unkingly roll of his eyes, Leortis added, "Well, aside from words of caution to always be careful what he promises to people."

Vicar barely managed to hide his surprise upon hearing Leortis's thoughtless words. The fact that an omega's word was damn near his bond was a carefully kept secret. After all, that knowledge in the wrong hands could cause trouble for omegas everywhere.

In fact, I'm surprised Charon's sire knew. Now I wonder who the hell he was.

"Why?" Regales asked, arching one dark brow.

"Ah. Well." Leortis smiled as he heaved a sigh. "That's something I probably shouldn't have mentioned." With a regretful look, he stated, "Let's just say, the power of the spoken word is especially potent when it comes to omega dragons."

"Cryptic," Councilman Shane Alvaro stated with a grin. The wolf shifter winked as he continued, "Which tells me it's something we really don't need to know." Shane relaxed back in his chair. "So, can omega dragons actually plan or know in advance when they're going to have their pup?"

"An omega does have that gift to a certain extent," Leortis revealed. "Due to the birthing line that appears on their abdomen, we'll know to within forty-eight hours."

Grinning, Shane stated, "Damn, my mate and I sure would have appreciated that ability." Barking a laugh, Shane admitted, "The waiting is the damned hardest part of having a little one."

Leortis grinned, nodding in understanding. "I understand perfectly. Leonidas was born from a female dragon, so we didn't have that ability, either." Shrugging, he told them,

"We'll be visiting Charon and his mate tomorrow along with Doctor Fulstat. As you're all friends, I'm sure he'll be passing along any news of timing after that."

"Glad to hear it." Lorian grinned broadly. "Charon and Dakota will make wonderful parents."

"That they will," Regales agreed, grinning. He rubbed his hands together. "It's been too long since the halls of shifter headquarters have rung with the patter of little feet. I hope more couples will be producing children soon."

Shane waggled his brows as he stated, "You and Theo could always adopt."

Vicar knew Shane was referencing Regales's human mate—Theodore Conway, Theo to his friends. Although, he had yet to meet the man.

Scoffing, Regales shook his head. "I'm too old to raise a child, and I know Theo has zero interest in that." Smirking, he peered over his shoulder at the guard who stood behind him. "I'll be like Dane, here. A doting uncle who can give the little one back when they start to stink."

Dane—who was Dakota's middle brother—snorted. "Not me. I'll just hand the little tyke off to Danny or Miggs," he claimed, referring to his own human mate as well as his older brother—Delanrue's—guinea pig shifter mate. Looking askance while shaking his head, Dane added, "Miggs has experience with that sort of thing and is actually looking forward to it. He's even got Danny excited."

"Sounds like Charon and Dakota will have plenty of help," Leortis stated, warmth filling his tone. "I'm happy to hear it."

Rising from his chair with a smile curving his full lips, Regales indicated the ending of the meeting without a word. "I'm meeting Theo in a few minutes in the cafeteria," he told them. "Would you all care to join me?"

While arching one brow, Vicar focused on Leortis. "Would you like to eat here or return to our lodgings?" They'd rented a large, lovely four-bedroom cottage which offered him, Warzer, and the mated pair plenty of room.

"Did I forget to tell you?" Leortis winced, looking guilty as he rose to his feet. "Cardin is getting a tour of the place from Theo. We should meet up with them at the cafeteria."

Growling under his breath, Vicar muttered, "Your highness, if I'd known that, I would have assigned Warzer to accompany him." He swallowed hard before murmuring, "What if something happens to him?"

"I assigned Priest, one of our best enforcers, to accompany them both, much to Theo's annoyance," Regales offered, moving to their side. "He won't allow anything to happen to either of them." His expression filling with pride, the grizzly shifter added, "Plus, my man's an ex-Navy SEAL. He can handle himself."

"Against a shifter, perhaps." Vicar didn't mean to question Regales, but he still felt plenty of urgency to get to the king's mate. "But what about a dragon?"

Shrugging, Regales grinned, not appearing at all upset. "Well, he also carries a tranq gun, so I think he'll be okay."

Leortis chuckled as he patted Vicar on his shoulder. "Come on, Vic. Let's go track them down." With a wide smile, he stated, "I know it'll make you feel better."

Vicar nodded. "It really would."

As head honor guard, Vicar was charged with the safety of not just his king, but the king's mate. He couldn't very well yell at Leortis in public, but once they were behind closed doors, his best friend was going to get an earful. Leortis shouldn't be pulling shit like this on him.

Fighting back his unease, Vicar did his best not to hurry Leortis and Regales as they made their way to the cafeteria. The hairs on his nape stood on end, and he felt a trickle of unease slither down his spine. Vicar even felt his dragon stir, and he worried about what he was reacting to.

Is something wrong with the king's mate?

6

Dane bumped Vicar's arm, drawing his attention. "It'll be fine," he assured softly, obviously catching on to Vicar's unease. "I happen to know that there are plenty of enforcers around who would be more than happy to step in and help if anything weird happens." Offering him a reassuring smile, the Komodo dragon shifter added, "We'll be there in a minute, and you'll see for yourself."

Sure enough, a moment later, Vicar followed Dane into the dining hall. He scanned the room, automatically searching for danger, but there was none. Vicar did see Cardin, however. The human was sitting and chatting with a dark-haired man while a massive black male lounged at the table with them, but the guy's eyes never stopped scanning the place.

Obviously Priest.

Relief filled Vicar as he followed Leortis toward the table.

Warzer touched the back of his arm before whispering in a nearly subsonic tone that barely reached Vicar, "I feel your pain, sir. The king would have torn the world apart if anything had happened to his mate."

Vicar dipped his chin in a barely perceptible nod of agreement. He watched Leortis stop at the table and bend at the waist. His king pressed a kiss to Cardin's lips, and his human welcomed the attention even as he blushed slightly. Vicar noticed Regales doing something similar to Theo, although their kiss appeared a bit more carnal, causing Vicar to look away.

When Leortis straightened, he continued to thread his fingers through Cardin's hair. "I'm going to get a plate of food, my love. Can I bring you anything?"

Cardin peered at Leortis through his lashes as he smiled up at the king. "I'd love some more tapioca pudding. It's really good."

"As you wish, my love." Leortis pecked another kiss to Cardin's lips before releasing him. Then he moved toward the buffet.

Following, Vicar glanced over the massive spread. There

were all sorts of offerings, from steak to lobster, with a variety of casserole and potato dishes for sides. He spotted the soup and salad bar, and his attention snagged on a container labeled *bread bowls*.

Vicar made his way in that direction. When he saw one of the soups offered was clam chowder, his mind was made up. After grabbing a plate, Vicar picked up a napkin-wrapped roll of silverware. Then he chose a bread bowl and filled it to the brim with the delicious-smelling chowder.

Watching Leortis head to the right where the dessert bar was, Vicar began pivoting to the left, toward the meal options. His tray crashed into something, and his fingers slipped along the edge. He scrambled, trying to right it, but even with his dragon reflexes, he still couldn't right the tray in time.

Vicar's full bowl of clam chowder toppled over the side . . . spilling all over not something, but someone. A man who'd obviously been refilling one of the soup vats stood there, his full lips having parted in surprise. He stared up at Vicar with wide, shock-filled brown eyes. Chowder dripped down his slightly pointed chin to plop onto his already-doused shirt.

Two things hit Vicar at once—the auburn-haired man was damn pretty—causing his prick to stir. Unfortunately, the second sensation won—mortification.

Embarrassment flooded Vicar, and while he knew he should apologize, he lashed out instead.

"Son of a bitch, you imbecile," Vicar snarled, glaring at the pretty man. "You can't sneak up while people are carrying food trays. What the fuck was going through that pea-sized brain of yours?" Sneering, Vicar added, "You must like getting dumped on to do dumb shit like that."

The man flinched just a little, causing Vicar's gut to churn uncomfortably.

"I'm so sorry, sir," the male stated quickly, even though Vicar knew it wasn't really his fault. Gripping the hem of his shirt, he began to slowly lift it over his head, obviously being careful to catch as much of the chowder as possible. "Just a sec. I'll make you another bowl."

Considering the male didn't mind getting undressed in front of others, Vicar pegged him as a shifter. When the guy revealed a lean, toned torso, he felt his blood flow south with a desire to explore that revealed flesh. Then the man removed the shirt entirely, taking most of the chowder scent with him . . . leaving behind just his own.

Oh, by the gods.

The sweet, masculine goodness of the fox shifter before him entranced Vicar's senses, and a ripple of need fired through his veins.

This is my mate.

Vicar's brain fizzled for an instant as he watched the man grab a fresh tray and begin dishing him up a new bowl of clam chowder. He couldn't tear his gaze from the beauty before him. Except, when the shifter turned back toward him, there was wariness in his brown eyes . . . and it hit Vicar like a fist to the chest.

Shit. I just cussed out my mate.

CHAPTER TWO

As far as days went, it wasn't the worst Desmond Takara had experienced. Still, getting cussed out by the sexy, handsome black man truly did suck. Fortunately, the clam chowder hadn't been that hot, so it didn't burn him or anything.

Desmond had been trying to move quickly, replacing the nearly empty vat of jambalaya with a new full one. The dish was always a hit when Chef Gage made it, so Desmond always kept an eye on it. Seeing the sexy, yet intimidating-looking male getting the clam chowder had distracted him a bit, and he hadn't ended up as efficient as he usually was.

Too bad the man's outward appearance doesn't match his inward one. He's a dick.

After getting said dick a new bowl of chowder, Desmond held the tray out to the man. He didn't understand the way the guy stood staring at him, not taking the tray. Desmond knew it couldn't be because he'd never seen a guy whip off a messy shirt before. After all, they were at shifter headquarters. For the most part, shifters weren't shy.

"I'm, uh, I'm really sorry for what I said," the man rumbled softly, finally taking the tray. "I shouldn't have lashed out at you like that." He rubbed a large black hand over his bald head, his full lips turning down into a grimace. "It was my fault. Will you forgive me?"

Confused as hell, Desmond stared up in shock at the man. He cocked his head, trying to understand why the man suddenly did a one-eighty. Needing to scent him, Desmond moved a step away from the food and the jambalaya still affecting his senses.

As soon as Desmond did that, a dark masculine scent teased his senses with an underlying hint of muskiness. The smell felt as if it wrapped around him, causing his mouth to water. Desmond's blood began to heat in his veins, and his prick took notice, plumping in his jeans.

Oh, holy crap balls.

Desmond stared wide-eyed at the big man before him. "You're my mate," he blurted out.

The man nodded. Holding out his hand, he stated, "I'm Vicar Rhomes."

Staring at the man's big hand, Desmond hesitated. He glanced around, seeing that they were the center of attention. Desmond also noticed that a number of shifter council enforcers were in the room, many of which he called his friends.

If this guy tries to pull anything, I have back-up.

While Desmond felt a niggle of guilt even thinking that, he already knew this guy had a temper and didn't have a problem displaying it. He didn't know if the verbal abuse would extend to physical. Even though the man was his mate, Desmond had to be careful.

Desmond reached out and slid his hand into Vicar's. "Desmond Takara."

The feel of Vicar's large calloused palm against his own caused goose bumps to erupt on Desmond's arm. Tingles washed up his limb. He felt his pulse speed up, and his gut bumped as if butterflies were inside.

Okay. So the chemistry is there.

Desmond realized that was a silly thought. Of course there would be chemistry with his mate. He'd been admiring him even before he'd officially met the man.

"It's so very good to meet you, Desmond," Vicar told him, his deep voice low and husky. After setting the tray aside, Vicar cradled Desmond's hand between his own and gave it a gentle squeeze. "Please, accept my apology. I'm not usually so . . . uh . . ."

While Vicar's nearly black skin hid a blush, Desmond could scent the man's embarrassment. Along with that embarrassment was a hint of annoyance and ire. Desmond knew Vicar was still upset . . . but he didn't know why.

Was it because he had to play nice now that he knew Desmond was his mate? Maybe he didn't want a male mate. Or perhaps it was because Desmond was a shifter?

Desmond had never seen or heard of Vicar before, and working in the kitchen and cafeteria allowed him to be privy to most gossip. He couldn't even pinpoint the man's scent beyond the fact that it was intoxicatingly delicious, and the man was his mate. Desmond knew he was a wary fellow, but he'd been in bad situations before and had vowed never to repeat those mistakes.

Not even for my mate.

His fox growled in Desmond's mind, clearly disgruntled by that thought.

We have to be careful.

Desmond reminded his fox of their time stuck in a cage, and his beast offered a mental whine.

When Desmond felt Vicar squeeze his hand again, he returned his attention to where it should be — the life-altering moment of meeting his mate.

"Uh, yeah," Desmond quickly stated, forcing a weak smile. "Apology accepted."

Accepted, but not forgotten.

Vicar smiled, appearing relieved. "I appreciate that, Desmond." He glanced at the nearly empty vat of jambalaya that Desmond had rested on the floor after pulling it out so he could refill the slot with the full one. Returning his intense, black-eyed focus to Desmond, Vicar surmised, "I assume you work here. Do you think you can take a short break to sit with me?" When Desmond hesitated, Vicar quickly added, "I'd really like the chance to get to know you."

Holding Vicar's gaze, Desmond felt his nipples bead. It might have been from the air conditioning flowing across his naked chest, but the more likely cause was from Vicar's continued scrutiny or the way he teased his thumb over Desmond's pulse point. Either way, it reminded him that he needed to change.

While shifters weren't prudes, working in the kitchen without a shirt wasn't the best idea.

Glad to have the excuse, Desmond shook his head. "I'm really sorry, Vicar. I should really get this vat back into the kitchen and track down another shirt." Desmond was pretty certain he had a spare in his locker, but he didn't mention that. Still, upon seeing the disappointed look on Vicar's face, he knew he had to offer his mate something. "Uh, I get off work in a couple of hours." Desmond glanced toward the clock. It was half-past noon. "At three o'clock," he revealed. "Maybe, uh . . ." Hesitating, Desmond thought of a safe place to meet the huge man before him. Then his brain supplied him with the perfect answer. "My friend, Delanrue, is having a barbeque tonight. If I give you the address, will you meet me there? We can sit, eat, talk, um . . . get to know each other?"

Vicar nodded once. "I would like that very much," he immediately agreed. "Where and when?"

"If you give me your phone number, I'll send that info to you."

Desmond attempted to pull his hand from Vicar's grasp, and for a second, he thought his mate wasn't going to let him go. With obvious reluctance, though, he did. Desmond pulled his phone from his back pocket and woke the device. As Vicar rattled off his number, Desmond input it.

As Desmond began to reach behind himself, intending to put it away, Vicar snatched his phone from his hand. Before he could comment, he heard a chime from inside Vicar's suit jacket. Then the man held it back out to him with a smile.

"There," Vicar stated, clearly pleased. "Now I have your number, too."

With a soft scoff, Desmond nodded. "Yup." He didn't know what else to say as he put his phone away. "Uh, so." Desmond took a step away, turning back toward the vat and the soiled shirt that he'd placed on top of it. "I'll, uh, talk to you soon."

Vicar reached a big hand toward Desmond's face.

Unable to help himself, Desmond flinched, uneasiness flooding him.

For a heartbeat, Vicar froze. His black eyes widened a smidge. His nostrils flared, and he tipped his head to the side just a little.

"I would never hurt you, my mate," Vicar rumbled, sounding a mixture of hurt and confusion. "Surely you know that?" As Vicar spoke, he finished the move and gently cradled Desmond's jaw. "You will be my heart and soul."

Desmond felt the warmth of Vicar's palm on his cheek, and his breath caught in his chest. Heat traveled down his neck, a mixture of pleasure and embarrassment. Nuzzling into Vicar's hold, just a little, Desmond tried to come up with a response that didn't make him seem like a fearful idiot.

"I guess I don't know." Desmond whispered the admission. Holding Vicar's gaze, he admitted, "I don't know you . . . or even what you are."

He still hadn't been able to place Vicar's scent.

"Well, we'll have to change that, then," Vicar murmured, caressing Desmond's cheek with his thumb. "I'm a dragon." Even as Desmond gasped upon hearing that revelation, Vicar continued, "And I know I didn't make a very good first impression, but we hold our mates in the highest esteem, too." Then Vicar eased a step closer to Desmond and bent close. He pressed a soft, chaste kiss to the corner of Desmond's mouth before whispering, "I look forward to easing your fears and learning everything about you, little fox."

Desmond stared, mesmerized, as Vicar straightened and took a step back. His hand fell away from Desmond's face, leaving a tingling warmth behind. Vicar smiled warmly at him, the look making Desmond's heartbeat trip in his chest.

"Until later today, then," Vicar offered, picking up his tray once more.

"Yeah," Desmond whispered. "Later."

Even though Desmond really wanted to know what a proper kiss from this man would feel like, he still picked up the vat, and the shirt with it, and turned away.

While Desmond's fox grumbled in his mind, he knew he needed to get away from Vicar. He needed a few minutes of quiet to process what had just happened. The man's presence was so very captivating, making it difficult to think.

I wonder if all shifters feel like that upon meeting their mate. Probably.

As Desmond used a shoulder to push open the swinging door that led into the kitchen, he couldn't resist glancing back. He spotted Vicar moving toward the buffet that held the meat and sides. The dragon—*wow, a dragon*—had been joined by another man, also large and in a suit. While Vicar had his head tipped, obviously listening to whatever the brown-haired guy was saying, his attention remained on Desmond.

When their eyes met, Vicar smiled once more.

Desmond couldn't help but smile back. His heart tripped in his chest once again, and he suddenly felt warm. Then he turned away and entered the kitchen.

"Saw what happened." Chef Gage immediately took the vat from him. As Desmond took the shirt off the top of the lid, the bear shifter asked, "You okay?"

Nodding, Desmond assured the hefty shifter that he was. "I'm okay. Was just shocked, is all."

"I was about to head out and bust the asshole's chops for speakin' that way to you," Gage told him, a low growl entering his tone. "Good thing he apologized."

Hearing that, Desmond felt the instant desire to defend Vicar. He didn't, though. The man had indeed acted like an asshole.

Instead, Desmond shrugged and started toward the locker room. "I think I have a spare shirt. Be back in a moment."

"Hey, I heard you say he's your mate," Gage called after him. "Do you want to take off after you clean up?"

Desmond paused and refocused on his boss. "No, thanks." Upon seeing Gage's surprised look, he admitted, "What I really need is to finish my shift. It'll give me time to think. To process this turn of events."

"You sure?"

Nodding, Desmond forced a tight smile. "Yeah. Thanks, though."

"Okay." Gage turned toward the garbage, probably intending to dump the soup dredges. "If you change your mind, let me know."

"Thanks," Desmond repeated, although he knew he wouldn't change his mind. While he figured it was a very human move—wanting to get away from his mate to process—he couldn't help it. Desmond struggled with change. It was why he was happy to work in the kitchen for over sixty years.

Ever since Priest helped me get away from—no, don't think about it.

As Desmond cleaned up a few clam chowder spots from his jeans, his thoughts turned to Vicar. Watching his friends find their mates, he'd mentally gone back and forth about what that would be like. A relationship would be a change, even one as wonderful as with his mate.

And now I've found him, and he's a dragon.

Desmond was impressed by that fact, despite himself. As he recalled Vicar's features, he couldn't say he was surprised.

The male stood around six-foot-six, had broad shoulders as if he could handle the weight of the world, and his suit only accentuated his thickly muscled body. When Desmond had first spotted him, he'd itched to rub his palms over his bald head.

Would he let me?

With a sigh, Desmond had to admit to himself that Vicar certainly wasn't what he would have expected in a mate.

Desmond suddenly recalled a comment he'd overheard. After finding his mate, Delanrue had been talking to his brothers, Dane and Dakota. The man had said, *Fate gives us the mate we need, not the one we think we want.*

In Delanrue's case, Desmond thought that was exactly right. The Komodo dragon shifter was a hard man who was the council's head interrogator. His mate, Miggs, was a guinea pig shifter who was sweet, kind, and exuberant about life. Delanrue was Miggs's champion, and Miggs reminded Delanrue of the joys of life.

Pulling on a fresh shirt, Desmond couldn't help but wonder.

Why does Fate think I need a hot-tempered dragon for a mate?

CHAPTER THREE

"Damn, Vicar," Leortis murmured into his ear. "What the fuck happened?" His king frowned a little as he eyed him, still speaking softly. "Can't remember the last time I saw your temper."

Vicar winced. "Yeah, that was bad." He had no excuse. "I was so damn embarrassed, and it just . . . fried my brain." Grimacing, Vicar glanced Leortis's way as they headed toward the table. "I can't believe I cussed out my mate."

"So he is yours?" Leortis asked for confirmation. After Vicar nodded, he smiled at him. Upon placing the tray on the table next to where Cardin was sitting, Leortis patted him on the shoulder. "Congratulations. Is he joining us for lunch?"

With a sigh, Vicar settled into his own chair. "Thanks, and no," he admitted. "He's finishing out his shift. Gets off at three." Vicar glanced at the clock.

Over two hours away.

Vicar was damn tempted to remain in the cafeteria all that time, hoping for the occasional glimpse of the man. He knew he couldn't, though. He had responsibilities, too. Plus, Desmond had asked for space to process.

Process what? We're mates? What's there to process about that?

Vicar had no idea.

"When are you seeing him again?" Leortis asked, picking up his knife and fork.

"This evening," Vicar answered. He eyed Dane, who was sitting beside Regales. "If fact, he just invited me to the barbeque at Delanrue's place tonight. So you know Desmond,

18

right?"

Dane nodded as he chewed his bite of steak. "Yeah, I know him," he confirmed after swallowing. "He's a good guy. You couldn't ask for a better mate." Then Dane scowled as he pointed his fork at him. "And you better watch that temper, man. Desmond deserves better than that."

Lifting his hands in placation, Vicar nodded. "You're absolutely right. It won't happen again." Grimacing, he claimed, "It shouldn't have happened this time. I'll make it up to him. I swear I will." Hearing Dane grunt and seeing him nod, Vicar felt relief that Dane accepted his word. As he cut into his own steak, he asked, "So, you're friends. Can you tell me about him?"

Vicar wasn't above getting the goods on his mate from another source. After all, he needed information to learn how to please his cutie. Standing at six-foot-six, Vicar couldn't wait to find out how Desmond's lean five-foot-eleven frame would feel pressed against his much bulkier one. Just thinking about it caused his blood to heat and his prick to begin thickening. But in order to get that chance, Vicar knew he needed to figure out how to make up for his abysmal first impression.

While Desmond had said that he forgave Vicar for his words, he knew better than to think the matter was forgotten. His mate most likely thought he was a mouthy hothead when, in fact, nothing could be further from the truth. Vicar was normally the strong silent type, always thinking before he spoke. As the head honor guard to the king, Vicar had to be.

So what a time to lose my temper.

"Well, I know he's worked here at the headquarters for over sixty years," Dane told him. Cutting into his baked potato, he went on to say, "His mother lives in the area, and occasionally, he misses our barbeques because she needs his help with something."

Vicar nodded slowly. "So he's close with his family. Siblings? Father?"

Dane shook his head as he chewed. "As far as I know, it's just the two of them." Smirking, he told him, "You'll need to make a much better first impression on her."

"Best foot forward with his mother. Got it," Vicar confirmed. "What's her name?"

Squinting, Dane hummed. "Ya know. Not sure," he admitted. Turning his attention to Regales, he asked, "Do you know Desmond's mother's name?"

Regales smiled. "Marisa Takara," he told them. "She'll be thrilled that Desmond's found his mate."

That's good news, at least.

Grinning, Regales told him, "You'll need to expect to have her move in with you, too."

For a few seconds, Vicar froze upon hearing that. "Package deal," he commented, processing that information.

"Very much so," Regales confirmed.

Vicar nodded slowly. After swallowing a bite of food, he commented to Leortis, "At least there's plenty of space."

"Indeed there is," Leortis agreed.

"Congrats, man," Warzer stated from Vicar's other side. "Your mate's a pretty man." The blond glanced toward the kitchen before frowning at his plate. "Damn jealous."

Growling, Vicar glared at Warzer. "Desmond is mine."

Warzer's blond brows shot up. Meeting Vicar's gaze, he lifted his free hand in placation. "I know, sir. I know." His lips curving into a wry smile, he admitted, "Just meant, I wanna meet my mate. That's all."

Vicar relaxed, surprised by his sudden spike of possessive jealousy. At over seven hundred years old, he'd been around the block a time or ten. Considering Dane had told him that Desmond had worked at the council headquarters for over sixty years, he figured the fox shifter wasn't some blushing virgin. In fact, the man's wariness of him bespoke of a rough past.

Gonna have to figure out how to earn his trust after my stupid display.

I'll figure it out.

"Do you know anything about his likes, dislikes?" Vicar returned his attention to Dane as he ate. "Hobbies? Interests?"

Dane smirked at him. "Trying to get a jumpstart on figuring out ways to woo him?" There was a teasing glimmer in the Komodo dragon shifter's brown eyes. "I approve." Sobering, Dane appeared thoughtful. "Well, he's a great cook." He indicated the buffet. "Obviously."

"He enjoys gardening with Charon," Regales added, glancing at him while scooping up a forkful of peas. "And he enjoys running in red fox form with Lorian's mate, Randy. He's a fox, too."

"So, cooking, spending time in the garden, and we'll need to have room for him to run as a fox," Vicar murmured absently, glancing at Leortis. His king smiled and nodded, silently telling him that they would make it work. Refocusing on the other two men, Vicar asked, "Anything else?"

"Well . . ." Dane drawled.

For the next fifteen minutes, Vicar did his best to pick the brains of the other men at the table. He needed every possible advantage after his epic fail. Finally, Vicar placed his silverware on the plate and leaned forward.

"When I reached for his face," Vicar began slowly, recalling his mate's nearly heart-stopping reaction. "He flinched . . . just a little. Do you recall any" — Vicar hesitated just a second, hating what he was about to ask — "abuse in his past?"

Dane, Theo, and Regales exchanged looks. As one, they started shaking their heads. Theo shrugged.

To Vicar's surprise, Priest spoke up for the first time. "Yes, but I'm not going to tell you about it," he stated bluntly. Crossing his arms over his thick torso, the dark male eyed him intensely. "I found out about it by accident while on another assignment. It's his story to tell." Priest's expression darkened. "Suffice it to say, the asshole who did it will never bother Desmond again."

Vicar wanted to demand answers, but he saw the hard resolve in Priest's dark eyes. He knew he wouldn't get anything from the man.

"How come I don't know about it?" Regales asked softly. The grizzly shifter had been on the council the longest, so he'd probably seen just about every report there was for the last hundred years.

Priest's black eyes narrowed just a smidge. "Like I said, I was on another assignment when I . . . helped Desmond." A tick flexed in his jaw, betraying his distaste for whatever had happened. "I didn't add it to my report because it wasn't relevant to my assignment."

Regales hummed softly as he nodded slowly. "I see." Inhaling deeply, he refocused on Vicar. "Well, the rest is up to you, Vicar. We all wish you the best of luck." Settling his arm along the back of Theo's chair, Regales added, "And if you need assistance, you know where to find us."

Vicar nodded as he thanked them. Turning to Leortis, he stated, "I'll need to bring in another couple of guards, since I'll be distracted. Do you have a preference, sir?"

Leortis groaned softly. "Very well." He narrowed his eyes as he peered out the window, obviously thinking. A moment later, he refocused on Vicar. "Kitoman is well-trained and always efficient. Other than that, I trust your judgment."

"Thank you, sir," Vicar murmured, honored by his king's words. "I suppose I'll see a few of you again soon."

Vicar had put in the request for Kitoman to join them, as well as another guard—Yeesom. Both men had been under him for over a century, and he trusted them to do their duty. That gave Vicar the opportunity to focus on wooing his mate.

To that end, Vicar found himself in the passenger seat of their SUV. Warzer was driving, and Leortis and Cardin were in the back. The new guards wouldn't arrive until the evening. Dragons couldn't very well be seen flying during the day. That meant Vicar wanted the king with him.

Plus, with the barbeque being at Delanrue's place, Vicar figured Charon and Dakota would be there. They still intended to be at Charon's check-up with Doctor Fulstat the next day. This just happened to allow them to get to know each other in a more relaxed setting.

Vicar felt a skitter of nerves rushing through him when Warzer turned the vehicle into a driveway. The dense forest had closed around them ten minutes before, and the trees towered over the drive. After a moment of rumbling over nicely grated gravel, they rounded a bend and a home appeared. While it wasn't large, it was definitely a nicely kept log-style structure.

A number of other vehicles were already parked near a detached garage. Warzer parked next to a blue sedan. Vicar slowly undid his seatbelt, taking a moment to inhale and exhale a couple of times.

Vicar was the last to get out, and he spotted a reassuring smile curving Cardin's lips when the human met his gaze. When the king had stumbled across the human at a barbeque, Vicar had been shocked. Still, the human male made Leortis happy, and that was all that mattered. While there had been a few grumblings from other dragons about the king's fated mate being human, those had mostly died off. After all, what did it matter? Leortis had already done his duty to the crown by providing an heir over a hundred years before.

"Come on, Vicar." Warzer patted him on the shoulder. "Time to go woo your man."

Vicar smiled faintly, his stomach still twisting as if there were butterflies within. He couldn't remember a time when he'd been so nervous. Even watching his king fight to keep his crown after mating with Cardin hadn't caused him such unease.

Girding up his courage, Vicar fell into step with the others. He could hear laughter coming from around the side of the house. The scents of grilling meats hung heavy in the air, as did the smells of a variety of shifters.

Amongst those was the heady scent of his mate.

Desmond is here.

Vicar's mouth watered with his desire to truly taste the fox shifter. The tiny hint of flavor he'd gleaned when he'd kissed the corner of Desmond's mouth, licking discreetly, hadn't been nearly enough. Vicar wanted to take Desmond into his arms, tuck him close, and truly ravish him.

His cock began to thicken at his thoughts, and Vicar reached down to quickly adjust himself.

Warzer smirked at him, and Vicar frowned back.

Then Vicar was rounding the corner of Delanrue's home, and he quickly cleared his expression. He didn't want Desmond's first look at him to be one where he was scowling at his fellow dragon.

Sweeping his gaze over the area, Vicar took in the dozens of laughing and chatting men, with a few women scattered amongst them. They stood in clusters of twos, threes, and more. Most held drinks of some kind in their hands. Others sat at tables, eating from plates of food.

Vicar spotted Desmond standing with Charon, Dakota, and another male he didn't recognize. Seeing the way the stranger rested his hand on Desmond's shoulder, he had to fight back a possessive growl. Vicar clenched and released his hands, trying to relieve the tension that shot through his shoulders.

How dare that man touch my mate.

"Take a couple of slow breaths and calm down," Leortis ordered, discreetly touching the small of his back. "Your mate knows he's yours. He's probably just a friend, maybe giving advice or reassurance, just like I'm doing for you."

Vicar obeyed his king. As he nodded, he did his best to relax. He knew he had to. He couldn't very well storm over there and yank the stranger away from Desmond. That certainly wouldn't make a good second impression, and he'd already botched the first.

Instead, Vicar glanced at the drink in Desmond's hand. His acute dragon eyesight allowed him to read the label of the beer bottle. Committing it to memory, Vicar moved toward the table holding the drinks.

I'll just take my mate a refill.

CHAPTER FOUR

"Uh, I think you should take your hand off my shoulder, Rigel," Desmond murmured, spotting the dragons — and Vicar in particular — as soon as they rounded the corner.

"Huh?" Rigel sounded confused. The friendly alligator shifter squeezed where he held him. "What's wrong?"

Desmond kept most of his attention on Vicar as he turned his head to speak with Rigel. He noticed the annoyed look flash across his mate's face before the big male managed to school his features. The bland expression Vicar pasted on his countenance wasn't fooling Desmond.

"I don't think my mate likes you touching me," Desmond explained softly, hoping his voice wouldn't carry across the yard. "For a sec there, he looked like he, uh, well, maybe wanted to rip your arm out of your socket."

"Your mate?" Rigel's handsome tanned face morphed into a huge grin. "You found your mate?" Instead of releasing Desmond, the shifter enforcer grabbed Desmond into a tight hug. "That's fantastic! Congratulations."

Desmond grunted as most of the air was squeezed out of his lungs. Tapping the big shifter's forearm, he hissed, "Air."

Rigel laughed while releasing him. "Sorry, man." He patted him on the back a couple of times before hooking the thumb of his free hand into a beltloop. "So." Looking around, Rigel asked, "Who is he?" before he took a sip of the beer he held in his other hand.

Figuring it was a good idea the bottle was glass, Desmond guessed Rigel would have crushed a can with that hug. "The huge black guy heading toward the drinks table," he told Rigel, tipping his chin in that direction.

Desmond couldn't help staring at the sexy man's ass in his form-fitting, black jeans. His fingers even twitched, and his mouth went dry. He quickly took several gulps of his beer to wet his whistle.

When Rigel began to cough, Desmond yanked his attention away from his handsome mate's form. Seeing the big shifter bent over, his free hand now resting on his thigh, as he spat beer on the ground, Desmond began patting him on the back. Charon stared at Rigel askance, while Dakota—who had his arm around his mate—chuckled as he eyed the other enforcer.

"Are you okay?" Desmond asked, worry filling him for Rigel.

"Yeah," Rigel responded, his voice low and rough. "Beer went down the wrong way." Wiping his mouth with the back of his hand, Rigel slowly straightened. His voice still sounded strained when he asked, *"That's* your mate?"

Desmond nodded.

Rigel looked shocked. "Do you know who he is?"

Glancing toward the drinks table, Desmond spotted Vicar handing a beer to the brown-haired guy who'd been in the cafeteria with him. "Uh, he introduced himself as Vicar Rhomes," he stated with a shrug before squinting at Rigel. "Why?"

"Vicar Rhomes? And that name doesn't ring a bell?" When Desmond shook his head, Rigel waved toward Charon and Dakota. "And they've never mentioned him?"

Rolling his eyes, Desmond heaved a sigh. "Well, you obviously know who he is. Wanna clue in the rest of the class?" Desmond didn't really mean to sound bitchy, but he was getting tired of Rigel's dramatics.

"No wonder he's got a possessive streak," Rigel stated, shaking his head. "That's Head Honor Guard Vicar Rhomes.

He's Dragon King Leortis's personal bodyguard and right-hand man." Rigel peered over Desmond's shoulder. "The man's a beast."

"A beast?" Desmond whispered, dread filling him. *Shit. What's Fate getting me into?* "Uh, what—"

"Not like in a bad way," Charon quickly cut in, lifting a hand toward him in placation. "Rigel means it as a compliment." The dragon omega pinned his hazel-eyed gaze on Rigel. "Right?"

"Oh, yeah, yeah," Rigel quickly confirmed. With a scoffing laugh, he told him, "I mean, you gotta be wicked smart, strong, and dedicated to end up the king's personal bodyguard." Grinning, Rigel continued with his hero worship. "Plus, he's head of all the guards. I mean, other than the king, he's like the most important dude in the dragon kingdom."

Well, damn.

Now Desmond really wondered what Fate was getting him into.

"Thank you for the kind words, shifter."

Vicar's deep voice came from behind Desmond, causing him to spin. The dark man smiled down at him, and if Desmond didn't miss his guess, he would say there was even warmth in his eyes. There was most definitely heated desire, and it created an answering bloom of arousal within Desmond.

Holding up the beer in one hand, Vicar told him, "I noticed what brand you were drinking and brought you a refill." He glanced at the beer in Desmond's hand, which was nearly empty. "For whenever you're ready."

"Thank you," Desmond murmured, surprised at the dragon's thoughtfulness. "I-I appreciate it." He quickly drained the last of what was in his bottle and set it on a nearby table.

"You're welcome," Vicar replied, handing it over. As he let

go, he teased his fingers along the sides of Desmond's, causing the hairs on his arm to stand at attention and his pulse to speed up. Vicar smiled, withdrawing his hand to indicate the men with him. "Allow me to introduce you to King Leortis, his mate, Cardin, as well as Honor Guard Warzer."

"Uh." Desmond's brain scrambled with the appropriate response. "I-It's an honor to meet you, Your Highness, uh, Your Majesty." As Desmond tripped over his words, he bowed his head and dipped at the waist.

"The honor is mine, Desmond," King Leortis replied. He touched the back of his head before sliding his hand to his shoulder and squeezing it lightly. "And no need for titles here. Not at a barbeque."

Popping his head up, Desmond tried to read the king's expression and his scent, gauging whether or not he was being sincere.

Gods, I hope this isn't a test.

King Leortis's smile appeared kind and welcoming, his stance relaxed with one arm wrapped around his mate's shoulders. "Really, no titles right now," he assured, perhaps reading the worry in Desmond's scent. "It's not often I get to relax at a barbeque, so just think of me as another regular guy."

Yeah, right.

Vicar rested his hand on Desmond's back lightly, rubbing up and down his spine in a soothing manner. "Leortis is one of my best friends. He speaks the truth. Consider this barbeque as being behind closed doors at the palace." He smiled warmly at Desmond. "I hope you'll end up having your own friendship, of a sorts, with him and Cardin." Vicar's smile turned wry as he told him, "The politics at the palace can get annoying at times, so it's nice to know you have people who have your back."

From those comments alone, Desmond realized Vicar expected him to move to . . . wherever he lived. As much as he figured that made sense, he found it annoying that Vicar didn't even bother asking. Forcing down his ire, Desmond offered the king a small smile.

"Thank you, sir." There was no way Desmond would ever feel comfortable calling the king by his first name. Smiling tentatively, he stated, "I'm honored."

Leortis grinned. "I suppose that's the best it's going to get at this point." Reaching out, the king squeezed Desmond's shoulder again. "I look forward to many years of friendship with you, Desmond." Then the king moved on, his attention moving past him. "Charon and Dakota." Leortis grinned broadly. "I'm so very honored to act as the second dragon in your birthing ceremony."

Charon gasped, his hazel eyes going wide. "You're going to help us . . . personally?" He glanced from Dakota to the other dragons, then back to the king. "I-I . . . wow," he stuttered, clearly shocked. His cheeks took on a pinkish hue. "Thank you, Your Majesty." Charon even tipped his head in obeyance.

Leortis groaned good-naturedly. "I just went over this with Desmond." Then he grinned as he stepped forward and squeezed Charon's shoulder, too. "If you can't manage Leortis, call me sir or sire or nothing at all."

Grinning, Charon peered at the king through his lashes. "Thank you, sir."

Grinning, Leortis responded, "Good enough." Then he lowered his focus to Charon's abdomen. "It's always fascinating how omegas barely show, even when they're almost due." With a twinkle in his brown eyes, Leortis admitted, "You would not believe the amount of bitching I had to tolerate with Leonidas's mother."

"I'll admit that the morning sickness sucked," Charon admitted, wincing and turning his attention to Dakota. "After I have this one, we're both going on birth control because I really don't want to have to use condoms."

Dakota grinned widely. "Deal, baby." Then the shifter dipped his head and pressed a firm kiss to Charon's lips.

"You know, I really want to be able to do that to you," Vicar whispered into Desmond's ear as he slipped his arm around his waist. Tucking him against his side, Vicar continued, "But you deserve a pseudo-date before I can expect that."

The way Vicar teased his fingertips under the edge of Desmond's shirt to feel the skin above his hip caused a shiver to go through him. Tingles spread up his torso and across his chest, causing his nipples to bead. Desmond bit his bottom lip, biting back a moan. He couldn't help the way his breathing caught in his chest upon feeling the sensual touch, and he certainly couldn't stop the fresh wash of arousal that surged through his body.

"Gods, but you do smell delicious," Vicar rumbled into his ear. Letting out a soft groan, he nuzzled his nose over the flesh of Desmond's temple. "Would you like to get some food with me?" Vicar purred into Desmond's ear, making the suggestion sound so much more provocative than it actually was. "We'll sit and talk. Share a little about ourselves, as well as our expectations for our mating."

Snapping his head to the left, Desmond peered up at Vicar. "Expectations?" He couldn't help but glance down at Vicar's full, dark lips. They were right there, after all, and he wanted to taste his mate just as badly as Vicar claimed to want to taste him. Still—"What do you mean?"

"Weeeell." Vicar drew the word out huskily as he flicked his attention to Desmond's mouth, reinforcing his claim in regards to his desires. "I know I made it sound as if I expect you to move to be with me, and I have to admit, that's true." Twisting his full lips into a grimace, Vicar told him, "You're my mate, but I'm head honor guard to the king. I'm needed there. I want to make the transition easy for you." With a squeeze to Desmond's waist, Vicar admitted, "I learned that your mother is important to you. Perhaps we can talk about what it would take to get her to join us?"

Surprise surging through him, Desmond yanked his focus off of Vicar's lips. He met Vicar's gaze once more. Seeing the seriousness within those black depths, he felt his heart skip a beat for a reason other than arousal.

"You asked about me?" Desmond questioned, nerves making his gut flutter. "About my mom?"

What else might he have learned?

"I asked those I was sitting with about your likes, dislikes, hobbies, and family," Vicar confirmed with a warm smile. "I wanted to know about you, my mate, find out what sorts of things we might have in common."

Desmond found his unease dissipating upon hearing Vicar calling him his mate. His fox practically purred in the back of his mind. He couldn't even begin to express how long he'd wished to hear someone call him that.

"Well, let's go get some food, then," Desmond replied softly. "We'll find a seat, share a meal, and some conversation."

"Sounds perfect." Vicar began guiding Desmond toward the tables near the grill.

Taking a chance, Desmond wrapped his arm around the larger man's waist. The corded muscle under his hand felt amazing. Desmond wished he could be as bold as Vicar and slide his hand under the man's long-sleeved polo shirt, but he just wasn't. Instead, he dreamed of the day when he would be able to touch the dragon's smooth flesh.

Huh. I wonder what he looks like as a dragon. I bet he's fierce.

After all, Vicar was the head honor guard.

"What's normally offered at these barbeques?" Vicar asked as they neared Delanrue and the grill. "Burgers and dogs?"

Wincing, he stated, "I guess I should have asked if I was supposed to bring anything. We're being really bad guests."

"Oh, the guys don't care about that," Desmond stated, trying to reassure his mate. "Bring something or don't. They always have more than enough of everything."

"The guys?" Vicar questioned. "Who are we referring to?"

"The Drudeson brothers." Delanrue answered for Desmond as he turned from his grill, tongs in hand. A small smirk curved his lips. "Dakota, Dane, and I rotate the barbeque at each others' houses. Our places are secluded and private." Delanrue used the tongs to indicate the forest around them. "Plenty of room to go for a run if guests are so inclined." Narrowing his eyes, he swept his gaze up and down Vicar's frame—not with interest, but assessing. "I bet you're bigger than Charon, so you may want to be careful if you decide to go for a flight."

Vicar's lips parted at the same time as the spicey scent of his surprise tickled Desmond's nose. "I could fly around here?" He sounded even more shocked than he smelled.

Delanrue dipped his chin in a slight nod. "Yep." His attention strayed across the yard to the group they'd left. "Although you may want to have Charon show you the boundaries before you and the king decide to go too far."

Vicar nodded slowly. "I'll keep that under advisement. Thank you." Then he turned his dark-eyed gaze on Desmond as he smiled. "But I'd like nothing more than to get a plate of food and sit with my mate, so we can get to know each other."

"You're in luck," Delanrue stated, turning back to face the grill. Although he did keep talking. "We have plenty. In fact, we even have ribs tonight. Charon had a hankerin,' and Dakota always delivers on his man's needs."

"It's nice to know that Charon's mate takes such good care of him," Vicar stated. His voice turned husky as he peered down at Desmond and rumbled, "I'll definitely have to take a page from Dakota's book so I make certain I treat my mate right."

"Yeah, after your initial introduction, you could use a few pointers," Delanrue stated bluntly, an amused snort escaping him as he glanced at them again. When Vicar arched one black brow in silent question, Delanrue smirked. "Dane was there, remember? My brother."

Desmond felt a wash of blood rush to his cheeks, and he grimaced.

Right. Bet our meeting is all the gossip right now.

"I'm sorry it happened that way," Vicar reiterated with a sigh. His smile appeared a little tight as he met Desmond's gaze. "So, what would you like to eat?"

Wanting to move past the awkwardness, Desmond focused on Delanrue. "What kind of ground meat are the burgers made out of today?"

On occasion, the brothers found a deal or went hunting, and Desmond never wanted to miss out on a chance to enjoy a game meat burger.

Delanrue grinned broadly, probably having expected the question, since Desmond asked it every single time. "Today, you get a choice. Buffalo, elk, or cow."

Desmond groaned. His mouth instantly began to water. "Elk, no cheese, with bacon," he requested.

"Great choice." Delanrue grabbed a plate off of a nearby table before opening the grill so he could fulfill Desmond's request.

As Desmond watched Delanrue place a patty, as well as several slices of bacon onto the plate, he hummed in anticipation. Hearing a soft growl from beside him, he snapped his attention up to Vicar's face. Desmond nearly lost his appetite for food when he spotted the hungry expression etched across the dark man's features.

When Delanrue asked Vicar what he would like, it took the dragon a couple of seconds to answer. Finally, he focused on the grill master and gave his order.

Desmond watched Delanrue place a massive rack of ribs onto the plate beside the burger and bacon. He knew Vicar would be using that plate, and he would get a paper one from the table for his burger. As they moved toward the table full of fixin's, Desmond focused on his breathing, trying to get the wild burst of arousal thrumming through him under control.

As Desmond fixed his burger bun, he couldn't help continuing to steal glances at Vicar . . . and each time, his dragon mate was staring right back at him, desire burning within the dark depths of his eyes.

Well, holy shit.

No way would he be able to gain control of himself with his mate watching him like that.

CHAPTER FIVE

As Vicar carried his large plate of ribs, creamy, buttery garlic mashed potatoes, as well as three heavily buttered dinner rolls, he couldn't help but eye Desmond's ass. The scent of his mate's arousal hung heavy in the air, and his mouth watered for something other than the delicious food on his plate. His dragon psyche urged him to skip the bullshit, grab the gorgeous fox shifter, and fly somewhere so they could complete the claiming.

In truth, Vicar wished he could do just that. Unfortunately, even though Desmond was a fox shifter and knew the score, he couldn't help but notice a few human-esque traits in the shifter's actions. While Vicar didn't think there was anything wrong with humans, per se — Cardin had been a champ about accepting and bonding with Leortis — Vicar hadn't wished for a human for himself.

While Vicar had gotten part of that wish, he still had to contend with whatever baggage was holding his mate back.

We'll get there.

With those words of encouragement to his dragon side, Vicar settled on a seat at a table. He noticed that it was located fairly close to where Charon and Dakota continued to chat with Leortis and Cardin. Warzer had wandered off, and a quick glance around found him chatting with the guy who'd been hugging and squeezing Desmond when they'd first arrived.

Desmond chuckled, drawing Vicar's attention. He saw that his mate was staring in the same direction. Unable to help himself, he arched a brow in silent question.

Carefully cutting his burger in half with a knife, Desmond glanced his way while smirking. "Well, it looks like Rigel is going to get a little action after all." Desmond snickered as he put down the knife and carefully picked up half the bacon elk burger. "It's been a while since he's picked up someone from one of our barbeques."

Vicar had noticed how Desmond had added mayo, ketchup, pickles, tomatoes, and lettuce. He'd watched discreetly so he would know how to make a burger to his mate's satisfaction in the future. While he was known as a hard man back at the palace—mainly due to his position, which forced him to be—he had no intention of that spilling over to his interactions with his mate.

"What do you mean by that?" Vicar asked, using a fork and knife to separate the ribs of the rack Delanrue had given him. The Komodo dragon shifter had been generous, and the slab before him was large and meaty. As he cut them, the juices oozed from the meat, making Vicar's mouth water with its succulence. Glancing up when he didn't get an answer, Vicar nearly moaned at the sight before him. Desmond's eyelids were at half-mast, his lips were curved up a little, and a blissful expression graced his beautiful features as he chewed the bite of burger he'd obviously just taken. "Damn, my mate," Vicar couldn't help but rumble. He sucked in a sharp breath, doing his best to control the desire racing through his body. "You eating is a stunning sight to behold."

Desmond blinked twice, swallowed, then met his gaze. His face flushed, turning him a lovely shade of pink. He ducked his head and peered at Vicar through his lashes.

Yup. Still stunning.

After a glance away, where Desmond set down his burger in favor of scooping a dollop of French onion dip onto a potato chip and popping it into his mouth, his mate returned his focus to Vicar. The pink was nearly gone from his cheeks, telling Vicar that the shifter had taken those few seconds to gain control of himself.

Too bad.

"Um, thank you," Desmond murmured softly before clearing his throat. He picked up his burger again. "So, um, that's Rigel. Rigel Patterson. He's an enforcer, an alligator shifter, and damn good at his job." With a roll of his eyes, Desmond added, "He's also a little bit of a man-whore." Lowering his voice, Desmond leaned toward Vicar and murmured, "Once the council accepted Councilman Regales Colearian's mating with Theo, quite a number of enforcers and guards revealed their bisexuality or whatever." Using his chin to jut toward Rigel, Desmond finished, "Rigel loves sex and is more than happy to engage in it with just about anyone . . . anywhere . . . as long as it doesn't interfere with his duties."

Vicar chuckled softly, nodding in understanding. "Nothing wrong with that, my mate." Waggling his brows, he whispered huskily, "I can think of a number of places in the castle that could be used for extracurricular activities." While seeing the way Desmond's face heated as his eyes narrowed, Vicar also noticed the peppery hint of jealousy in his mate's scent. *Mmmmm . . . very nice . . . except, I don't want my mate getting the wrong idea.* With a half-shrug as he picked up a meaty rib, Vicar met Desmond's gaze as he murmured, "At least, according to Leortis. He tells me he and Cardin enjoy each other whenever the mood strikes." Wincing, he mumbled, "Says the spontaneity helps keep the spark alive, whatever that means."

To Vicar's relief, Desmond snickered. "I understand what he means."

Nodding slowly, lifting the rib to his lips, Vicar asked, "Perhaps you could explain it to me?"

Desmond once again blushed oh-so-prettily.

"Sure, I will," Desmond murmured, peering at him

through his lashes. "Eventually."

Then Desmond took a big bite of his burger and moaned.

Vicar had to bite back his own similar response, but for an oh-so-different reason. His mate's noises were so very difficult to ignore. Still, it wasn't as if Vicar could ravish his mate right there in the middle of the group of shifters. Truth be told, Vicar wouldn't want to, either.

I want my mate's moans, sweet words, and body flushed with passion all to myself. No one else should ever see.

Deciding a subject change was in order, Vicar asked, "I know you've been working at Shifter Headquarters for over sixty years. Have you worked in the food industry all that time?"

Desmond's shoulders lost their bit of tension, telling Vicar he'd made the right choice. "I have," his mate admitted with a smile. "It may sound boring to others to do the same thing for so long, but I love creating food." Smiling wryly, Desmond quickly added, "I'm not a chef like Gage or a baker like Miggs, but I'm damn good at cooking."

"I believe you," Vicar hurried to assure. If his fingertips hadn't been covered in barbeque sauce from the delicious ribs, he would have reached over and squeezed Desmond's wrist. Instead, he shared, "There's nothing wrong with doing the same thing for years on end." Vicar shrugged as he smiled at his pretty fox. "After all, I've been Leortis's head guard since shortly after he took his position as king. That was nearly three hundred years ago."

"Wow." Desmond whistled appreciatively. "That's a long time. No wonder you consider him your best friend."

"We grew up together," Vicar admitted. "My father was Leortis's father's head guard. I was training for the position from the time I could lift a sword."

"Huh." Cocking his head in a very canine manner, Desmond commented, "I wouldn't have thought you dragons would use swords."

Vicar chuckled. "Well, back then, we didn't have firearms. Although, over the centuries, we have incorporated certain ones into our training."

"Back then," Desmond mumbled around a mouthful of food. After swallowing, he asked, "How long ago is *back then*?" Desmond cleared his throat and shifted in his seat. "Uh, is it okay to ask how old you are?"

"Truth be told, I've lost count over the years," Vicar admitted. Seeing the surprised light fill Desmond's eyes, he quickly explained, "I've weathered over seven hundred winters. Somewhere in the neighborhood of seven hundred and thirty-five, give or take a couple of years."

"Damn," Desmond whispered, his pretty brown eyes widening. "That's—" He paused and roved his attention over Vicar's features and frame before meeting his gaze once more. "You look . . . great." Then Desmond furrowed his brows. "Uh, I guess I don't actually know how old dragons normally live for. Are you like gargoyles? A couple of millennia? Older means stronger and wiser and such?"

Vicar hummed, thinking about that question. "Well, the oldest dragon I've heard of was a mage dragon, and if the tales are true, he lived to be nearly four thousand years." Upon seeing Desmond's jaw sag open, Vicar quickly added, "But the average dragon is not quite that long-lived. Twenty-five hundred to three thousand years is average."

"That's a big average to have," Desmond whispered, his expression turning vacant as his thoughts turned inward. When he remained silent for a moment, Vicar opened his mouth to offer a penny for his thoughts, but then Desmond spoke again, his soft words barely carrying to Vicar over the chatter of those around them. "Possibly fifteen hundred to two thousand years together. Wow. I-I hope y-you're not—" Desmond seemed to realize he was talking out loud, for he snapped his mouth shut as a tinge of embarrassment crept into his scent. Peering at Vicar out of the corner of his eye, Desmond murmured, "I hope we like each other beyond the sexual chemistry."

While Vicar knew that wasn't what Desmond had originally intended to say, he let it go. He figured it was something that wasn't too flattering to him. After all, Vicar had been an ass during their first meeting.

Considering Priest's warning, Vicar guessed it would take a little time for his mate to get past that.

But we will.

"I'm certain we'll find things in common, Desmond." As Vicar did his best to assure his fox shifter, he set down his last rib bone — they'd been delicious — and picked up his napkin. "Although I look forward to exploring this amazing chemistry that I feel between us." After cleaning his hands, Vicar reached over and gripped his mate's wrist. Gently rubbing over the pulse point, he felt Desmond's heartrate pick up and smiled at that reaction. "Like many paranormals, I've never been in a relationship before. Just never wanted anyone beyond a night or two." Holding Desmond's gaze, Vicar hid none of the desire he felt for the lean shifter sitting next to him. "You are different, my mate. You will be the heart and soul of a dragon, and I'll do my damnedest to prove I'm the man you need, too."

"Thank you, Vicar," Desmond replied quietly. "I don't mean to make you jump through hoops."

Desmond twisted his wrist, pulling away from his grip. Vicar felt a stab of surprised disappointment at the move, but it was immediately replaced by pleasure when Desmond threaded their fingers together. Vicar returned Desmond's smile, feeling an odd sensation of satisfaction at simply sitting and holding hands with his mate.

"We'll find our way," Vicar assured. He lifted their twined fingers and kissed the back of Desmond's hand. "We're paranormals, my mate. It won't take all that long."

For several seconds, they just sat staring at each other, and Vicar basked in the warm regard of his mate.

Then Desmond blinked, and a fresh blush swept up his cheeks. He glanced down at his plate before grabbing his beer and taking a swig. After returning his bottle to the table, Desmond refocused on Vicar.

"So."

Desmond cleared his throat, and Vicar waited patiently for his shifter to gather his thoughts. In fact, he felt a wash of pride that a few soft declarations could obviously mean so much to his mate. While Vicar wasn't a man who shared his emotions or feelings often, he made a mental note to do just that with his mate, and often.

"So where do you live, anyway?"

Vicar felt his brows shoot up at the unexpected question. He smiled as he relaxed in his chair, still holding Desmond's hand. Pleasure filled him that his mate never attempted to pull away.

"I guess I did forget to cover that, huh?" Vicar grinned when he saw Desmond arch one brow in silent inquiry. "The dragon king's home, and by extension my home, is hidden in the Poconos in Northeastern Pennsylvania."

Desmond appeared surprised. "You are?"

Vicar nodded once. "We are."

His look turned to one of confusion. "I thought the Poconos was a tourist destination. Gorgeous area for hiking, fishing, skiing. Stuff like that."

"Indeed it is," Vicar confirmed with a chuckle. "And you would not believe the business our people do running swanky lodges as well as tourist boutiques and eateries."

"But how do you keep yourselves secret?"

"Humans rarely see what they don't want to see. Few believe dragons ever existed anymore, regardless of all the myth and legend created around our kind," Vicar revealed with a squeeze of Desmond's hand. "That means no one actually looks for us. There are about four hundred of us living in and around the area, and we own a lot of property, giving us a buffer against public lands." Vicar saw Desmond begin to slowly nod, processing that information. He continued explaining, saying, "Plus, we have people in law enforcement, park rangers, and search and rescue. We keep a close eye on where humans may be hiking and camping, so we can share with everyone where the safe fly zones are."

"What about radar and tracking?" Desmond leaned forward, clearly interested. "Aren't you afraid of being spotted by a satellite or something?"

"Something in the metallic composition of our scales hides us from any known tracking devices," Vicar explained after a discreet glance around. With a tense smile, he added, "So far, anyway."

Vicar hoped all those in the area who might overhear him were allies. If that sort of information got to the wrong people, dragons could become hunted for their scales. They didn't generally share the information with outsiders, but Desmond was his mate, and he wanted to be truthful with him.

Obviously picking up on his unease, Desmond squeezed Vicar's hand. "Your secrets will be safe with us."

Sighing, Vicar nodded. "Thank you."

Gotta have faith in Desmond's friends.

"Vic!"

Upon hearing Leortis's call, Vicar leaped to his feet, drawing Desmond with him. He peered around frantically, his attention landing on his king. As Vicar hurried toward him, he took in the panic upon the countenance of the usually stoic man.

"What's wrong?" Vicar asked, stopping before him.

A second later, Warzer joined them, still buttoning his jeans and smelling of Rigel and sex.

Guess Desmond was right.

"Charon is having the baby."

Upon hearing Leortis's declaration, Vicar gaped. He jerked his attention to Charon, who rested one hand on his abdomen while sporting a pained expression. Dakota had his arms wrapped around his mate protectively.

"Now?" Warzer asked incredulously. "I thought you weren't due for another week or so."

Charon shrugged. "I'm bonded to a shifter, not a dragon." He grimaced as he was hit by another contraction. "It's now."

Vicar remained frozen for another couple of heartbeats. Then he swung into action.

CHAPTER SIX

Desmond watched in fascination as Vicar took charge. Pointing at Warzer, Vicar ordered, "Find Delanrue's mate, Miggs. Tell him we need blankets, hot water, and clean cloths." As Warzer hurried off, he turned to Desmond. "Will you notify Delanrue and Dane that their brother's mate is in labor? I'm certain Dakota would appreciate his brothers' support." A smirk curved Vicar's lips as he looked Dakota's way. "He's looking a little green around the gills, so to speak."

After a glance at Dakota, Desmond saw exactly what Vicar meant. The normally smiling, happy-go-lucky shifter appeared pale. His brows were furrowed, and worry gleamed in his green eyes as he stared at his mate.

Desmond nodded. Turning, he quickly scurried away, knowing that finding Delanrue would be easy enough. He still stood at the grill.

"Del," Desmond called, mentally wincing when the huge man turned and pinned him with a narrow-eyed stare. Only a select few called him by the shortened version of his name, and Desmond had certainly never tried to take that liberty before. Still, Desmond pushed aside his worry at possibly having offended the massive enforcer and told him, "Charon's in labor." Seeing Delanrue's eyes widen, Desmond pointed across the clearing where he'd left Charon and Dakota. "Do you know where Dane is?"

"Not off hand," Delanrue admitted even as he roved his gaze over the area, obviously looking for him. "I'll track him down," Delanrue told him as he spotted Warzer talking to a wide-eyed Miggs. "What's he doing?"

"Asking for things," Desmond admitted, dancing from foot to foot. "Uh, you know. Water, blankets, and other stuff."

Delanrue jerked a nod. "Help them. I'll find Dane and meet you back at my brother."

Desmond nodded and quickly rushed after the pair where they were entering the house. Evidently, the other guests had picked up on the sudden change in the air, for they all quieted. They glanced around, trying to figure out what was going on. Desmond didn't take the time to share.

Instead, Desmond found Miggs in the kitchen, running hot water into a pot. "Take that when it's ready," the guinea pig ordered before moving toward the hallway, leaving Warzer with the task of carrying what would probably end up being a heavy pot of water.

Smart man.

"What can I carry?" Desmond offered, following Miggs.

Miggs opened the hallway linen closet before pointing toward the guest room. "Grab the comforter and throw blanket, as well as all the pillows you can carry." Then Miggs began piling towels of different sizes and colors into his arms.

Desmond quickly moved to obey. Entering the guest room, he spotted the blanket folded at the foot of the bed. After tossing that over his shoulder, he gripped the comforter and yanked it free, bundling it up and tucking it under one arm. Finally, Desmond scooped up a pair of pillows.

As Desmond hurried out of the room, he mentally winced. The items were nice, soft, and of good quality. They were also sky blue. Desmond couldn't imagine getting blood from a birthing out of them.

Desmond had never been present during a birth. If he were asked, he would have to admit that he'd never wanted to be, either. The idea of watching a baby being expelled from between a woman's legs . . .

Just, yuck!

He'd always been damn happy he was gay, and he'd never lain with a woman in his life.

Still, for the opportunity to see a baby dragon, Desmond couldn't resist sticking around. Even though he'd worked with Charon in the kitchens for nearly a decade, it wasn't until the last six months that he'd begun to really become friends with him. While Charon had been under a spell disguising him as a human, he'd been reclusive and shy.

These days, Desmond enjoyed joining Charon in the gardens on occasion. While he wasn't as passionate about it as the omega, he found it fun. Desmond really enjoyed sharing in Charon's exuberance for it.

They'd talked quite a bit in the gardens, becoming friends. He knew that Charon was carrying an egg. What Desmond had never asked was if, after the egg hatched, would it be a dragon or a babe?

Considering Charon was bonded with a shifter and not another dragon, it was possible that his friend wouldn't have even been able to answer that question.

Anticipation filling him—along with a fair bit of stomach-churning butterflies—Desmond returned to Charon's side. Both Delanrue and Dane were already there, as was Danny. With the way Danny hung back, looking a little pale, Desmond thought the human had a mindset similar to his own.

"Here's the blankets and pillows," Desmond offered, holding them out to Vicar, who still appeared to be in charge. The king was too busy holding Charon's other hand, offering soft words of encouragement. "Where should I spread them?"

Vicar smiled warmly at him as he took one of the blankets. "These will do nicely to wrap around Charon and Leortis after they shift back. Thank you, my mate." He took the comforter, too, setting them aside.

While Desmond didn't completely follow, he simply nodded. "And the pillows?"

"Uh." Vicar stared at them blankly for a moment. "I don't recall asking for pillows." With a shrug, he took them anyway. "We can make Charon more comfortable until he needs to shift."

Gaping, Desmond took a step back. He was going to see his friend shift? Excitement filled him, beating back his slight queasiness. Desmond had only seen Charon shift once before, and he'd thought it was amazing.

So very cool!

Desmond watched as Vicar helped Dakota situate Charon on the ground, sitting on a pillow with his back between Dakota's spread thighs. Dakota rested his back against Delanrue's legs, his brother offering support. Dane knelt to Dakota's left, resting his hand on his brother's shoulder. Danny and Miggs hung back, arms around each other.

King Leortis crouched to Charon's right. Even as he held Charon's hand with his left hand, he used his right to unbutton his dress shirt. At some point, while Desmond had been gone, Leortis had removed his jacket. Cardin flanked the king, and Warzer stood at the human's side, clearly guarding him.

"I put in a call to Doctor Fulstat, but there's no way he'll arrive in time," Vicar told everyone softly. "But he's promised to stay on the line, just in case any problems arise."

Dakota snapped his attention to Vicar. "Do problems arise often?" he asked, panic creeping into his voice.

"No," Vicar assured, shaking his head. "I can't remember the last time I've heard of a dragon omega having trouble birthing." With a reassuring smile, Vicar added, "It actually goes much smoother for them than it does our females."

Delanrue squeezed Dakota's shoulder, getting his attention. "And I called Doctor Bulgazi," he stated calmly, referring to the doctor that worked out of shifter headquarters. "He's on his way and should be here within twenty minutes."

Staying out of the way, Desmond glanced around. Evidently, everyone had realized the gravity of the situation.

They were quiet, only occasionally whispering between each other. They were seated far enough away to offer a modicum of privacy while being close enough to offer aid if they were needed.

Gods, I hope no help is needed.

Uncertainty filled Desmond, and he wondered if he should go sit with them. He took a step backward, thinking to do just that. Desmond wasn't really family, after all.

Vicar reached back from where he knelt near Charon's thigh and grabbed Desmond's hand. He smiled up at him. "Stay," he encouraged softly. "This is a blessed event. I would love to share it with you, my mate."

Desmond squeezed Vicar's hand back and nodded. When Vicar released him, he wrapped his arms around himself and waited. To his pleasure, Danny and Miggs moved close to him and wrapped him in their hug. Desmond was only too happy to return their embrace, offering what emotional support he could.

"Dakota." Vicar pointed at Charon's shirt. "It's time for you to take Charon's shirt off. Let's see how far along his labor is."

With obviously gentle hands, Dakota eased Charon's shirt from his body. He immediately rubbed his palms over his mate's arms. Keeping one latched onto Charon's upper arm, he skimmed the other palm down his lean torso.

The difference in Charon's appearance after the spell still amazed Desmond. For years, Charon had appeared to be a five-foot-six, blond-haired, blue-eyed twink. In actuality, Charon's build was extremely similar to Desmond's own—standing five-foot-eleven with a wiry, toned build. Charon's hair was actually a pretty auburn, and his eyes were hazel. Of course, as was the way with mates, Dakota hadn't given two shits about what Charon had looked like after the spell had been removed. He'd just wanted his mate happy.

Desmond looked at Vicar, wondering if his mate would

have acted the same. Would he have cared if Desmond had looked different? He figured it was a moot point, and he pushed the thoughts away.

It didn't matter, and Desmond was just being ridiculous.

While waiting, anticipation made him a little jittery, but Desmond fought the desire to bounce from foot to foot. He watched Vicar reach for Charon's midsection. With his palms hovering over the slight bulge, showcased by the deep red horizontal line across Charon's lower abdomen, Vicar peered at Dakota.

"Do I have permission to touch Charon, Dakota?" Vicar asked solemnly.

For a second, Dakota just stared at him with furrowed brows. Then he nodded slowly. "Yes."

Vicar smiled and nodded slightly before returning his attention to Charon's abdomen.

Dakota glanced up at Delanrue questioningly.

A second later, Leortis answered the silent query. "Dragons are extremely territorial when it comes to their pregnant partners," he stated softly. "It's why this is normally done only by family members." With a small smile, Leortis continued, "Vicar asked for permission because if you'd been a dragon, and he's not kin to you, you might have felt compelled to shift and attack him."

"Okay," Dakota responded simply. Quirking up one corner of his lips, he pressed a kiss to the side of Charon's head before muttering, "Still got things to learn about your kind, baby."

Charon tipped his head back and to the side, peering up at Dakota with a loving gaze. "We haven't been together long."

Dakota's color began to return as he smiled back at Charon. "Not nearly long enough." Then he pressed a chaste kiss to his lover's mouth.

Feeling a little like a voyeur, Desmond lowered his gaze to

what Vicar was doing. He almost wished he hadn't. His mate appeared to be palpating the red line on Charon's stomach.

As Vicar worked it, the flesh would separate a little, but not completely. There were tendrils still keeping it together. When the sides came back together, it almost appeared to be a gooey substance oozing within.

"Oh, god," Danny whispered, and Desmond felt the human tuck his face against his neck.

"It's okay," Miggs whispered, rubbing Danny's back. "I think that's normal."

Vicar had obviously heard him, for he glanced their way and smiled. "It's normal. Everything is progressing as it should be."

Even as Vicar spoke, another wave of pain hit Charon, and he groaned softly. The gap Vicar kept working grew wider. The tendrils became thinner.

"Almost there, Charon," Vicar assured, smiling up at him. "You're going to feel the urge to shift soon. Don't fight it." He peered around at everyone. "Be ready to move out of the way."

Right. Charon is much larger in his dragon form.

Watching with bated breath, Desmond knew he wasn't the only one who practically vibrated with anticipation. He felt Miggs's arms tighten around him. Upon hearing Danny grunt, Miggs's grip loosened as he whispered an apology.

Yup. Someone's excited.

When another wave of pain hit Charon, it was followed by a hard shudder.

Vicar pulled his hands away from Charon. "Back up," he ordered as he leaped to his feet. Vicar wrapped his thick arms around all three of them, urging them away from Charon.

At the same time, Desmond noticed Delanrue and Dane doing the same to Dakota. Warzer was pulling Cardin back, too. Leortis, however, stayed close and also began to shift.

"That's the way, Charon," Vicar encouraged as Charon's

dragon rose to his feet. "Now, just relax and let nature take its course." Vicar pointed to the towels and ordered Dakota, "Move in with the towels, Dakota. Prepare to catch."

Dakota gaped. "Me?" He practically squeaked the one word.

"You're his mate," Vicar reminded. With a shrug, he added, "I could do it, but I think as the sire, you should be the one."

"Dakota," Charon rumbled, his dragon's voice deeper and rougher than his human one. "Please, my mate. It's time."

Dakota quickly got moving. He grabbed a thick towel from the ground where Miggs had left them. Spreading it out, Dakota rushed to Charon's side.

Even as Desmond waited, he couldn't help admiring Charon's dragon. The beast was a beautiful metallic, light-purple color. He had a long-tapered snout and elegant neck. His hazel eyes had darkened to an amber color and shown with intelligence. Charon's arms had lengthened, transforming into wings, and were currently bent so he rested his weight on what was essentially his elbows.

A huge dark-blue head drew close to Charon's smaller purple one and nuzzled against his cheek. Unable to help himself, Desmond gasped softly. He heard Danny doing the same.

While Charon's dragon had to be double the size of an elephant, Leortis's dragon was even larger—probably double the size again. He had sharp horns on his head over his eyes, and his scales were the deepest of midnight blue. There were spikes on his tail. Instead of his forearms being wings, Leortis had massive appendages lifting from a point just below his shoulders on either side of his body.

"Damn," Miggs whispered.

Vicar chuckled softly. "Yup. That about sums up our king."

"Almost there, little one," the dragon king rumbled, his deep voice practically vibrating the air around them. "Let your little one out."

With a soft grunt, Charon seemed to obey. The scales of his belly pulled apart, and an oblong orb a bit larger in size than an ostrich egg slipped into the towel. Dakota immediately cradled the vibrantly colored egg in his arms, a look of wonder on his face as he stared at the swirls of deep green and pale purple.

"Rest the egg on the ground and step back, Dakota," Vicar ordered softly.

Dakota seemed to startle. He glanced around, noticing the two dragons watching him expectantly. With a grin, he settled the egg, towel and all, on the ground. Then he took several steps backward.

As one, Charon and Leortis let out a small concentrated stream of fire. The flames licked around the egg, and the smell of burned cloth filled the air. A second later, a soft wail reached their ears, and both dragons immediately cut off their flames.

Vicar released the three of them. He quickly grabbed another towel and rushed forward. From within the circle of charred fabric and grass, he picked up a tiny dragon with green scales tipped in pale purple. Almost instantly, the dragon morphed into a human babe. It opened its mouth and let out a mighty cry.

Grinning broadly, Vicar wrapped the towel around the infant as he headed toward Dakota. Holding out the bundle, he told him, "Congratulations. You have a little omega boy."

Dakota's grin stretched his lips so wide that Desmond didn't know how his face accommodated it. He took his son and clutched him to his chest. Staring at his son, he moved closer to Charon, who was still in dragon form.

Vicar eased backward a few steps, and that was when Desmond saw it—a gleam in his eyes.

Something Desmond hadn't even known was there eased

in his chest.

If my mate can tear up from a baby's birth, I know I can trust him to be a good man.

CHAPTER SEVEN

Sadly, even a dragon couldn't keep their clothes intact when they took their true form.

That was why Vicar had asked for the blankets. He held one up, ready to wrap it around Leortis as soon as he returned to human form. He noticed Delanrue doing the same for Charon. Dane was too busy cooing at the baby.

The love evident on all three of the brothers' faces caused a lump to form in Vicar's throat.

That baby is going to be so well cared for.

Turning away from the beautiful sight, Vicar swallowed hard. He caught Desmond's eye and smiled at his mate. The warm smile his mate returned caused his gut to twist for a new reason.

Oh, wow. I like the way he's looking at me.

"I'll take that," Cardin murmured, plucking the blanket from Vicar's hands.

Vicar snapped his attention back to the matter at hand. Seeing his king crouching in human form, he silently cussed a blue streak. Out loud, Vicar offered, "I'm sorry, Leortis. Was caught woolgathering."

Leortis snorted as he tugged the blanket that Cardin draped over his shoulder tighter around him. "You mean you were caught admiring your mate." Smiling widely, Leortis rose to his feet, tucking the comforter around him as he did so. "There's nothing wrong with that." Using one hand to hold the blanket in place, Leortis wrapped his other around Cardin, holding him close. "Go to him, Vicar. Your work here is done. I'll make the necessary calls to the doctors. Doctor Fulstat can walk Doctor Bulgazi through the process of checking over a dragon babe."

"Thank you," Vicar replied gratefully. After a dip of his chin in deference to his king, he turned and headed toward Desmond. Reaching him, Vicar couldn't resist wrapping his arms around him and pulling him close. "Well?" he asked softly. "What'd you think of that?"

"That was absolutely amazing," Desmond replied quietly, staring up at him. He rested his palms on Vicar's chest, rubbing his thumbs over his pectorals. "Thank you for asking me to stay close."

Vicar nodded once, Desmond's touch making thought difficult. Although he'd only just met the man, he knew he never wanted to be without him. He couldn't imagine anyone fitting against him so perfectly or having another's touch cause such a riot to his systems.

Desmond was hardly doing more than resting against him, but Vicar's nipples quickly beaded. His gut clenched with heat and desire. Blood rushed to his groin, warming him from the inside out as his prick thickened behind the fly of his jeans.

Finding his tongue, Vicar managed to rumble, "In general, dragons have a difficult time getting pregnant." He slid a hand up to tease his fingertips along the column of Desmond's neck. "The fact that Charon did so swiftly is a testament to Fate's blessing."

To Vicar's surprise, Desmond smirked. "Or Dakota's potency."

Vicar chuckled as he nodded. "Or maybe Charon's fertility."

"Fate's blessing or not, we're on birth control," Dakota declared, interrupting them. He grinned widely as he held a human-looking Charon tucked against him. His mate held their new babe in his arms, and both men beamed at Vicar. Dakota glanced at Charon and the babe he held before pinning a grateful look on Vicar and saying, "Thank you so much for your help and guidance."

"It was truly my honor to assist you," Vicar replied, a smile softening his dark features. "We'll have to remember to take into account slightly skewed timelines should other dragons find their mates among shifters." Vicar glanced toward Danny, who was in Dane's arms while talking quietly to Miggs. With a shrug, Vicar amended, "Or humans or others."

"Can dragons get their male fated mates pregnant?" Danny asked suddenly, glancing between them. "Or is that just a gargoyle thing?"

As Danny had asked the question, Desmond had stiffened in his arms. "That's just a gargoyle thing," Vicar responded, rubbing up and down his shifter's back. "Only omega dragons can get pregnant." Vicar smiled at Desmond, appreciating that his mate immediately relaxed against him once more. "Sorry, babe. No babes in the cards for us."

"While I certainly wouldn't want to be the one to carry it, that's really too bad." Desmond returned his smile. "I bet you'd make a great father." Then his brows furrowed as he glanced toward Leortis before once again meeting Vicar's gaze. "Unless you already have some?"

Vicar understood to what Desmond alluded. Leortis had sired a child with a chosen female dragon in order to produce an heir. Vicar had never had any desire to do that.

"No, my mate," Vicar shared. "I've never sired a child." Recalling Desmond's first words, he couldn't help but smile. "But thank you for thinking I'd make a great father."

"There's always surrogacy," Leortis teased, stopping beside them. Before turning to coo at the babe, he smirked and added, "After all, who's going to take your place as head honor guard for Leonidas?"

Shaking his head, Vicar smirked at his king. "That ship

sailed a long time ago." Leonidas was already over a hundred years old, not to mention he had a couple of best friends who were more than worthy and capable of the position once the time came. "I think Leonidas will have a difficult time deciding who to give my position," Vicar admitted. "Llaudsa or Znyrda."

"You may be right on that one," Leortis replied, nodding knowingly as he stepped closer and allowed Dakota, Charon, and the others to move off so they could show off their new babe to everyone else. "Both would make a fine head honor guard for him."

"Could they share the position?" Desmond asked, glancing between them. When all eyes fell on him, he pressed against Vicar, silently seeking his support. Vicar wasn't entirely certain Desmond was even aware he was doing it, but Vicar loved it. His voice much softer, Desmond murmured, "Or isn't that allowed?"

Vicar hummed, rubbing his palm up and down Desmond's back once more. "Interesting idea," he offered, smiling at his mate. "I don't think that's ever been proposed before." Vicar focused on Leortis and arched a brow in silent question.

Leortis hesitated a few seconds before shaking his head. "No, it hasn't," he confirmed. Tipping his chin up, he hummed softly. "But I can't recall any laws against it, either. Just because it hasn't been done before doesn't mean it can't happen. I think I'll mention the idea to Leonidas." Grinning widely, Leortis added, "Fresh ideas are always welcome."

"Don't let some of the elder dragons hear you say that," Vicar stated with a grumble. "They're stuck in the dark ages."

With a sigh, Leortis nodded grimly. "They are. Fortunately, they don't come around a whole lot, and they can rarely agree when they do." Squeezing Cardin against him a little, Leortis focused on his mate. "I think it's time to find me some pants. I should have had the presence of mind to strip to my boxer-briefs."

"The kind of underwear you favor is a bit more than I wanted to know about my king," Warzer teased, arriving and holding up a pair of pants. "Compliments of Delanrue."

"Ah, thank you." Leortis grinned and began moving toward the forest, Cardin still in his hold. "I'll be back soon."

"But not too soon, right?"

While Cardin whispered the words, Vicar still heard them. Unable to help himself, he smiled just a bit.

"Absolutely not too soon," Leortis confirmed. Then he added, "Grab my jacket. It has what we need."

Vicar grimaced as he peered toward the starlit heavens. He really hadn't needed to know that his king always carried around the necessities to fuck his mate. Of course, considering how Leortis said he loved carnal moments of spontaneity with Cardin, it made sense.

I wonder if my mate will enjoy that sort of thing.

Returning his focus to Desmond, Vicar suddenly found his head filled with the image of his shifter's hands pressed against a tree. He would have his ass pressed back into Vicar's questing hands. Vicar would hold him steady as he plunged into his inviting hole over and over until —

"And here are some sweats for you, Charon," Delanrue rumbled, handing them over. Then he turned to Vicar and crossed his arms over his chest. "Maybe you and Desmond would like to take a trip into the woods, too?" His eyes narrowed as the left corner of his mouth quirked up. "You can go for a run and . . . see what pops up."

Vicar growled softly. "Not happening. I'm claiming my mate in a nice soft bed." Then, realizing he should ask about that kind of stuff, he focused on Desmond. Even though he noticed the way his fox shifter nibbled his bottom lip and his face had turned a light pinkish hue, Vicar still offered, "We can go for a run, if you'd like." Seeing his mate's face grow even darker, Vicar quickly added, "Nothing has to happen other than letting your fox out." He couldn't help himself as he added, "I'd love the chance to play a game of chase."

I'll just have to remember that that doesn't mean I get to claim my prize at the end if he's not ready.

Damn. That'll be difficult.

As Vicar held Desmond's gorgeous brown-eyed gaze, he realized something else.

For my mate, I'll do it. I'll do anything.

"I really do want to see your dragon, but I really want a bed, too," Desmond told him, and Vicar resigned himself to a chase without a prize at the end. Then, to his surprise, Desmond lowered his chin and whispered, his voice turning sultry, "But we can play chase another night, too. Do you need to stay with your king? Or can I take you home with me?"

Vicar sucked in a harsh breath, and his prick flexed within the confines of his jeans. Even his breath caught in his throat.

For all the world, Vicar wanted to believe what he thought Desmond was asking for — was offering.

Does my mate want me to come home with him? To fuck? To breed? To consummate our bond?

Vicar couldn't get anything resembling those words past his throat.

Why the sudden turnaround?

With a nibble to his bottom lip, Desmond heaved a sigh. He looked away. His expression appeared blank, but his scent gave away his true thoughts.

Disappointment. Nearly debilitating embarrassment. Profound sadness.

"Um, I'm sorry if I overstepped —"

"I want you so damn bad, I don't even know how to put it into words." Finally, Vicar managed to get words rushing past his throat. Seeing Desmond gape at him, Vicar barely managed to resist laying a deep kiss on him so he could thrust his tongue between those parted lips and taste him properly. Instead, Vicar dropped to one knee and gripped Desmond's slender waist to hold him in place. "My sweet mate," he whispered huskily. Running his other hand up his shifter's side, teasing under his shirt, he felt the warm, firm flesh beneath and the way his soon-to-be lover's abdominals clenched and released in reaction to his touch. "Yes. If I understand what you're asking, to take me home with you and complete our bond, I'd be the happiest fucking dragon in the galaxy."

Even as Vicar knew his words weren't the most eloquent, he still couldn't help how much he loved the huge smile that spread across Desmond's slightly pointed features.

So fucking sexy.

"I know I've been a little human-like wrapping my brain around my connection, and I'm sorry for that," Desmond began.

Needing his mate to understand that that didn't matter to him, Vicar hurried to tell him, "I don't care about that. You could have taken weeks, and I would have found a way to wait."

And I won't add how much I would have tried to constantly seduce and change his mind.

"I don't want to wait," Desmond declared. His lips curved into a knowing smile as his brown eyes heated. "And I know you don't either, my dragon." Gripping Vicar's wrist at his waist, Desmond tugged, urging him upward. "Let's go. I want to touch you, to feel you touch me, and to bond us."

"Yessssss," Vicar hissed, more than on board with that.

As Vicar allowed Desmond to lead him around the house to the vehicles, he satisfied himself with the knowledge that Warzer was there to guard the king. Not only that, there were dozens of shifters, too. Just in case, even as Vicar followed Desmond's urgings to climb into the passenger seat of his *Jeep*, he pulled out his phone and texted Delanrue's address to Guard Kitoman and Guard Yeesom. He imagined they would be able to get there before too long.

Shoving his phone into his pocket, Vicar focused on Desmond as he fired up his vehicle and drove them away.

Soon . . . oh-so-soon . . . I will bond with my mate.

Vicar practically vibrated in his seat.

CHAPTER EIGHT

Other than the desire burning through his body, Desmond couldn't even guess what had come over him. Well, other than the undeniable need he felt for his mate. Desmond was a shifter, after all, and not in any way immune to the potent urges of the mate-pull.

Plus, Desmond really didn't want to be. While his mate represented change, if he were truthful with himself, he'd always wanted that special someone.

And now, I have him.

Desmond nearly moaned upon scenting the heavy, masculine fragrance of Vicar's arousal. He saw the way his dragon flexed his fingers where they rested on his thighs. Desmond wondered what those huge hands would feel like upon his skin.

Delicious, I bet.

"T-Tell me why you ch-changed your mind."

Upon hearing Vicar's deep, rough voice, Desmond nearly jerked the wheel. It was so damn sexy. *He* affected this massive, amazing male like that.

Then the actual request registered, and Desmond tried to piece together an acceptable answer.

"Desmond?"

Realizing he was taking too long, Desmond admitted, "I thought you were sexy-as-fuck when I saw you making your bowl of soup." He hurried on, not giving Vicar time to comment. "The jambalaya I was carrying dulled my senses so I couldn't smell you." Scoffing, Desmond glanced Vicar's way as he eased to a stop at a sign. "Then the whole soup-dousing debacle. You scared me. I realized who we were to each other. I thought I needed time."

Gods, that was such a silly response. Fate wouldn't make a mistake like that.

Except, it happened.

"You worried I was an abusive asshole, like someone from your past."

Desmond winced as he started them forward again. "Yep. I let my past experiences cloud my future, and I asked for time to process." Driving steadily, Desmond reached over, gripped Vicar's hand, and squeezed. "You gave me that, for which I'll forever be grateful, but after seeing you help give birth to Charon and Dakota's little boy, I realized my fears were unfounded."

"Fears?" Vicar flipped his hand and squeezed Desmond's hand back. "I never mean to cause you fear. So please, tell me which action or actions caused it, and I'll do my best never to repeat them."

A giggle erupted from Desmond upon hearing Vicar's sincere words. "I know. I get that now." He squeezed Vicar's hand back. "I worried your yelling meant you were abusive."

"Shit," Vicar hissed, bowing his head. His entire body language betrayed how crestfallen he felt. "I'm sorry. I'd never purposefully hurt you." His dark-eyed gaze found Desmond as they paused at another stoplight. "Physically, mentally, or in any other way."

"I know. I know that now," Desmond assured, drawing Vicar's hand to his lips to press a light kiss to his knuckle. The honk of a horn encouraged Desmond to continue forward, and he returned his attention to the road. "And I'm sorry that I allowed my past and my fears to delay what we already knew was coming, to act as if I was going to deny the gift Fate was giving, not just to me, but to you."

Finally, Desmond pulled into his driveway, and he parked

beside his small, two-bedroom cottage. After turning off his vehicle, he turned to face Vicar more fully. "We're a couple. We're made for each other. Even not yet bonded, I feel the way my soul cries out for you." Reaching out, Desmond only hesitated an instant before he rested his palm on Vicar's shaved jaw. "The way my fox cries out for your dragon. I want you." Holding Vicar's dark-eyed gaze, Desmond admitted, "I *need* you. Can we find a way to be together?"

"Most definitely, my sweet fox," Vicar responded, sounding so very sincere. His dark eyes smoldered as he held Desmond's gaze. Resting his hand over Desmond's on his jaw, he turned his head just enough to kiss his palm before rumbling, "Nothing would give me greater joy than twining my life with yours."

Desmond's heart thudded in his chest, and a shudder of need worked through him. The hairs on his arm stood on end, and the skin of his palm tingled. He flexed his fingers, sliding them along the smooth flesh of Vicar's strong jaw.

Gathering his courage, Desmond whispered, "Then let's head inside."

"With pleasure," Vicar responded, his voice deep and rough. "I'll follow you, my mate."

Then Vicar squeezed Desmond's hand lightly before lowering it. He drew away from him, turning toward the door. When Vicar opened his door, the cool evening air yanked Desmond out of his admiration of Vicar's strong frame easing from his *Jeep.*

Desmond grabbed the keys from the ignition and hurried to follow. Rounding the hood, he cast a smile Vicar's way before starting up the walk. When Desmond reached the front door, he felt Vicar crowd in behind him, his big body warming him from behind.

With his fingers trembling, Desmond struggled to get the key in the lock. He felt Vicar nuzzle his nose against the side of his neck, sniffing deeply, and nearly dropped them. When Vicar's large hands settled on Desmond's hips, he groaned and gripped the keys tighter.

"Having trouble," Vicar teased, pressing sucking kisses along the column of Desmond's throat.

"Yep," Desmond replied, because honestly, he couldn't very well deny it. His mate's touch made thinking nearly nonexistent. Vicar nipped at the tendon where Desmond's neck met his shoulder, where Desmond desperately wanted him to leave his claiming bite, and groaned deeply. "I-If you wanna g-get in the h-house tonight, you n-need to stop."

Vicar growled against his neck. "Don't want to." Still, he did. Vicar straightened, although he didn't back up. Instead, Vicar reached around Desmond and gripped the hand with the keys in it. "Here," Vicar offered, steadying it, before helping Desmond insert the key into the lock.

Finally, Desmond managed to unlock the door and lead the way into the house. Vicar tugged the keys from Desmond's hand as he followed him closely. Desmond noticed his dragon toss them onto the side table before closing and locking the door behind them.

Desmond took the opportunity to put a little bit of space between them . . . just enough to catch his breath.

Except, Vicar didn't seem to want that. His dragon reached out a long arm and grabbed his wrist, reeling Desmond back to him. He wrapped his second arm around him as soon as he could, tucking him tight against his chest. Once more, Vicar lowered his head and nuzzled his neck.

"You smell so damn good, Desmond," Vicar rumbled, sniffing noisily before licking him. "Taste amazing, too. Want to lick you everywhere." After nipping his neck once more, Vicar rumbled, "Where's your bedroom, little fox?"

Moaning at Vicar's ministrations, Desmond could barely form the words. "To the right," he murmured breathlessly.

"End of the hall."

Vicar hummed in answer.

Then Desmond found himself swept off his feet. He barely held in his *eep* of surprise upon finding himself carried bridal style. On instinct, Desmond wrapped his arms around Vicar's neck and clung as Vicar moved swiftly through his home.

The door to the bedroom was open, and Desmond winced upon spotting the unmade bed. Not to mention, he'd left a towel on the floor from his shower, and there were clothes draped over the back of a chair from when he was trying to decide what to wear to the barbeque. A clean freak, Desmond was not.

Vicar didn't even pause. He settled Desmond in the middle of the unmade bed. With a tug, Vicar yanked the side of the comforter and top sheet out from under him and pushed them to the bottom of the bed.

"I need you, my mate," Vicar growled, reaching for the laces of Desmond's hiking boot. He made quick work of removing it, as well as the sock, before doing the same with the next. Then Vicar reached for the fly of Desmond's jeans. "Tell me I can have you."

Finally, Vicar paused, his fingers hovering close to Desmond's fly, as he peered up at him.

Desmond's cock throbbed, and he wanted to feel those hands — so close yet so far — on him in the worst way. "Yes," he replied simply. Grabbing the hem of his shirt, he tugged it upward. "Hell, yes." Desmond yanked the fabric from him before tossing it over the side of the bed.

"Yesssss," Vicar hissed in response. He quickly opened Desmond's fly, revealing his weeping, needy erection. "Beautiful," Vicar crooned.

Crooking his fingers, Vicar skimmed the backs of the first two up the underside of Desmond's straining erection. The move sent tingles through his shaft, settling pleasantly in his balls. Groaning, Desmond sucked in a sharp gasp as his prick jerked and bobbed. He trembled, gripping the sheet beneath him as he struggled to control his hips.

"Gorgeous," Vicar growled, his eyes dark with desire as he peered down at him. Gripping the edges of his jeans, he peeled them down Desmond's legs. "Tell me," he demanded, dropping the jeans on the floor and reaching for the hem of his own shirt. "If I'm moving too fast."

Then Vicar whipped his shirt over his head, revealing his broad, thickly muscled torso.

"Not too fast," Desmond panted, staring at all the muscled dark skin on display. He wanted to touch, to explore, desperately. "In fact, hurry up."

Vicar chuckled gruffly as he dropped the shirt on the floor. "Your wish." His hands immediately went to his fly. "My command."

In short order, Vicar shed his clothes.

Desmond groaned in appreciation. The man before him was the epitome of masculine beauty. His tall, heavily built frame rippled with muscle, but he wasn't oversized like a bodybuilder. Sweat already gleamed on Vicar's flesh, telling Desmond of the man's need. His black erection jutted from a nest of barely-there curls—long, thick, and uncut. His foreskin was already half-retracted, showing a wide flushed head and the gleam of pre-cum threatening to pool in his slit.

Desmond licked his lips, wanting to taste so damn bad.

Vicar groaned, gripping the base of his prick. "See something you like?" He growled the words as he prowled forward, so much the predator.

"Oh, yeah." Desmond saw no reason to deny it. He wanted this man before him, this dragon, his mate. Yanking his gaze from the spectacular vision of maleness before him, Desmond met Vicar's gaze. "I wanna suck you so damn bad. Bet you taste better than you smell."

A feral grin curved Vicar's lips, betraying that his eyeteeth had already begun to sharpen and extend in anticipation of claiming him. Desmond realized he even saw the gleam of the dragon's eyes peering down at him, betraying just how close to the surface the beast was. Relief and a fresh burst of arousal rushed through Desmond upon knowing just how much Vicar wanted him, too.

"Where's your lube, Desmond?"

Unable to get words past his too-dry throat, Desmond answered by deed. He half-rolled to the right and reached for his nightstand. After a quick dip into a drawer, Desmond came away with his prize, holding up the lube for Vicar to see.

"Perfect," Vicar rumbled, crawling onto the bed. He grabbed it from Desmond's hand, then levered over him, bracketing Desmond's head with his forearms. "Before I let you suck me, there's something else I want first."

Staring up at Vicar, his face only a few inches away, Desmond lifted his hands and settled them on his mate's sides. "What's that?" he asked softly, enjoying the way his much larger mate's expression suddenly became heavy-lidded just from that light contact.

"A kiss."

Upon that declaration, Vicar lowered his head. He sealed his mouth over Desmond's own. Vicar nipped at his bottom lip, urging him to open, and Desmond had zero desire to deny him. Desmond quickly parted his lips, welcoming Vicar's questing tongue.

Desmond groaned as Vicar's masculine essence burst across his taste buds. His mate's flavor consisted of a hint of beer, the ribs, the barbeque sauce, and beneath that, something all Vicar's own. It was deep and robust, masculine and heady, and caused Desmond's need to join with this man to rise even higher.

Sliding his arms up and around Vicar's back, Desmond

gripped his mate tighter. He urged him to come closer, to lie on top of him. Desmond desperately wanted to feel Vicar's flesh against his own. Arching his body, he tried to get skin-on-skin.

As Vicar's tongue dipped and teased, mapping Desmond's mouth, his left hand moved to Desmond's shoulder, then down his arm. The dragon moved his palm across Desmond's torso, pausing to pluck at a nipple. Then he moved on to map Desmond's side, stomach, and abdominals, exploring his body as he plundered his mouth.

Finally, *finally*, when Vicar's hand landed on Desmond's hip, his mate lowered against him, pressing their bodies together from shoulder to thigh.

Desmond turned his head, breaking the kiss. Groaning wantonly, he rocked underneath his mate. With their size differences, Desmond's erection rubbed across Vicar's ripped abdominals in the perfect of ways. He felt the bump of Vicar's cock head against his balls, then below as it slid along his trench. When his mate's cock nudged at his hole, he hitched a leg around Vicar's lower leg and rocked with him, urging him to increase the pressure.

"Fuck," Vicar snarled, pulling away from him. His dark eyes gleamed with a feral intensity as he muttered, "You're not ready, baby." Lifting up, Vicar heaved a deep breath before adding, "Need to get your ready." Then he smirked. "And you promised to suck my dick."

Licking his lips, Desmond lowered his gaze to Vicar's thick shaft. His mouth watered. He hummed appreciatively, knowing his dragon's erection would be more than a mouthful.

"You're killing me," Vicar said on a groan. "Need you so damn bad."

"Then come up here," Desmond urged, trying to tug at Vicar's shoulders, not that he could budge the huge man.

To Desmond's surprise—and disappointment—Vicar

drew away. "What?" he began.

Vicar swung around, moving to straddle Desmond's head.

Desmond found his attention riveted to the gorgeous masculine length and dark heavy balls dangling oh-so-enticingly close. When Vicar gripped the base of his shaft and pointed his prick down toward his mouth, he quickly opened. For a few seconds, his mate used his hold to skim his damp crown across Desmond's bottom lip, painting it with his pre-cum.

Unable to help himself, Desmond flicked out his tongue to lap it up. The ever-so-mild flavor still managed to cause his taste buds to zing. On his next lap, Desmond caught the edge of Vicar's crown, and the man's warm flavor burst across his tongue, yanking a groan from him.

The deep sound of Vicar's growl answered Desmond.

Needing more, on Vicar's next teasing pass, Desmond gripped his mate's thighs. At the same time, he lifted his head and clamped his lips around his mate's crown. He eased his tongue under his foreskin to lap deeply at the leaking slit as he sucked strongly on Vicar's swollen flesh.

Vicar barked a cry, the sound filled with ecstasy. His body arched, pushing more of his length into Desmond's mouth. He started to withdraw, only to half-thrust again.

Desmond moaned, vibrating Vicar's shaft, reveling in the knowledge that he was making this big, powerful man lose control, even if just a little.

"Gods above and below, baby," Vicar snarled, continuing his short, jack-rabbit thrusts. "That's the way. Fuck, that's perfect."

Grinning around his mouthful of meat, Desmond dug his fingers tighter into Vicar's thick thighs as he hung on for the ride, doing his best to blow his mate's mind.

CHAPTER NINE

Vicar nearly lost his mind to the bliss Desmond was providing. The wet sucking heat encasing the top half of his cock felt better than any deep-throating blowjob he'd ever received in the past. His brain fritzed with the bliss of it, and he feared he would blow right that second.

Managing to peel open eyelids he didn't recall closing, Vicar forced himself to recall his plans.

Right. Prepare my mate.

Although Vicar couldn't remember the last time he'd gone down on a guy, he still focused on Desmond's bobbing, weeping dick before him. He knew he wanted a taste of that. Plus, Vicar needed to distract Desmond from the expert fellatio he was giving his cock.

After pouring a healthy dollop of slick onto the fingers of his right hand, Vicar closed the bottle and set it aside. He inserted his other hand between Desmond's thighs. To his gut-clenching pleasure, his mate opened with barely a press.

Vicar's attention was instantly riveted on the pretty pink hole he desperately wanted to plug. Adjusting his position a little, he gripped the base of Desmond's erection. The move drew a gasp from his lover even as it pulled his prick a little out of Desmond's mouth, offering him a touch of relief.

Doing his best not to overthink it, Vicar wrapped his lips around Desmond's crown. His mate's flavor burst across his tongue, and he hummed appreciatively. As Vicar enjoyed the slightly sweet nectar of his mate's pre-cum, he realized he could get used to doing this often.

My mate tastes so damn good.

Vicar thought it was almost as good as the taste of his mouth. Desmond shuddered and rocked beneath him, his hips jerking spastically. His legs trembled, their movement drawing Vicar's attention back to his waiting hole.

Moving his slicked hand, Vicar pressed one thick digit against Desmond's hole and pushed. His finger was immediately swallowed in tight heat. As his mate squeezed his finger, he imagined sinking his prick into that heat, and he couldn't help his groan.

Desmond answered with a whimper while lifting his hips, rocking his prick deeper into his mouth as he pushed against Vicar's hand.

Reading the signals easily, Vicar knew what his mate wanted—needed even. He eased his finger out partway, touched a second finger to his hole, and eased that one in beside the first. Vicar began to finger-fuck Desmond, crooking his fingers . . . searching.

With a shout, Desmond turned his head, releasing Vicar's erection. His body jolted beneath him. The fingers on his thighs tightened nearly to the point of pain, betraying the intensity of Desmond's enjoyment just as much as the spurt of pre-cum that filled his mouth.

Vicar quickly swallowed the fluid before popping off his mate's cock. He swung his leg over his mate's head, pulling from his grip. He admired Desmond's slack-jawed expression and deeply flushed face, neck, and chest.

As Vicar adjusted their positions, he never stopped finger-fucking his mate. He bumped his prostate with nearly every pass. By the time he got into position, Vicar had three fingers stretching Desmond's ass, and his mate took them beautifully.

Made just for me.

With a growl, Vicar began to stretch out over Desmond, needing inside his mate in the worst way. Looking down, he took in just how much smaller his mate was compared to him. He paused, even stilling his fingers. With his clean hand, Vicar traced his fingertips along Desmond's jaw.

Desmond blinked up at him, his pupils widely dilated with lust.

Vicar smiled, loving that look. "You ready for me, baby?" he asked softly. "You ready to be mine forever?"

"Already yours," Desmond replied softly, his words ever-so-slightly slurred. His smile appeared almost drunken. "Ever since you poured soup on me."

Groaning, Vicar fought his urge to roll his eyes. "Thanks, but you really were in the wrong place at the wrong time," he muttered, unable to help but chuckle when Desmond snickered. He grinned at the levity. He couldn't remember the last time he'd bantered with a lover. Wiggling the fingers still embedded in Desmond's chute, Vicar teased, "But now, you're in the right place at the right time. You ready?"

Desmond clamped onto Vicar's fingers, yanking a groan from him. "I'm so ready," he told him, reaching up to grip Vicar's shoulders. "Claim me."

Vicar moaned, wanting to do that more than anything. Still, he had to offer, "I'm a big man, Desmond. Would you be more comfortable on your hands and knees this first time?"

Narrowing his eyes, Desmond shook his head. "No, I want to see you. Need to, really." He nibbled his bottom lip for just a second before admitting, "So I can claim you, too. I-Is that okay?"

With his dragon roaring approval in his mind, Vicar issued a feral growl. "Hell, yeah. That sounds damn perfect."

"Then, please." Desmond managed to open his legs a little bit wider. "Please, my mate. Claim me," he repeated.

"Never need to beg, my mate," Vicar assured. "I'll give us both what we need."

Easing his fingers out of Desmond, Vicar rocked onto his

knees. He grabbed the lube and squirted a healthy dollop directly onto his jutting shaft. Feeling the slight chill, Vicar hissed, but at least it helped him calm just a smidge. He really didn't want to blow as soon as he got in his mate, but he feared he was dangerously close to doing just that.

After swiping over his cock, spreading the slick, Vicar leaned up. He grabbed a pillow from the top of the bed. Desmond seemed to know exactly what he was thinking, for he planted his feet and arched up. Vicar took the invitation and shoved the pillow under his mate's hips.

With Desmond's ass raised invitingly, Vicar slid his palms up his thighs. He teased at his shifter's groin with the fingertips of one hand while wrapping his lubed fingers around his man's long, slender erection. Jacking him slowly, Vicar couldn't help but admire the perfectly proportioned swollen flesh. He figured it was a nice slender eight inches, and for just a second, he wondered what it would feel like in his ass.

Vicar didn't bottom . . . but for his mate, he just might consider it.

Hearing Desmond's moan, reveling in the sound of his mate crying his name, Vicar dismissed the random thought. He released his mate's cock and quickly slotted into position. With the base of his dick in hand, he guided his crown to Desmond's prepared hole.

Gripping Desmond's thigh in his other hand, Vicar lifted his mate's leg higher, spreading him even wider. He nudged at his shifter's opening, testing it. Feeling the muscle give, Vicar thrust.

The muscle gave way, allowing him entrance.

Vicar groaned deeply as he watched Desmond's body swallow his crown. The tight squeeze enveloped him, threatening his control. His balls tingled, and he fought back his urge to buck.

Desmond hissed, jerking Vicar's gaze to his mate's face. He

saw the pinched line of his brow and the way his nostrils flared. Reaching for Desmond's erection again, Vicar once again began to jack it.

"Breathe for me, baby," Vicar urged between gritted teeth. His abdominals clenched as he fought his body, forcing himself to stay still. "Just breathe and relax."

"Gods," Desmond muttered, blowing out a breath. "You're huge."

"I'll fit," Vicar assured. "I promise."

I'll also make sure I work him up to four fingers next time.

"I know you will," Desmond panted. "I was made for you."

Vicar smiled up at his lover, his own tension fading just a little. "Yeah, you were."

The pressure around his knob eased just a little, telling Vicar that Desmond was relaxing—that he was getting used to his intrusion.

Desmond blew out a slow, deep breath. "We're good now. Thanks for pausing."

Holding Desmond's gaze, Vicar murmured, "You're my mate, Desmond. I'll always strive to make it good for you."

The sweet smile Vicar received in response to his claim caused Vicar's heart to trip for a reason completely different than the intensity of the need burning through his veins.

Just damn. How'd I get so lucky?

Desmond flexing his chute muscles redrew Vicar's attention to where it should be—claiming his mate. He snapped his focus back to Desmond's face. His mate grinned at him.

"There you are." Desmond's brows furrowed just a little. "Where'd you go?"

Vicar gave his mate a broad smile, hoping the affection he felt filled his expression. "Just wondering how I got so damn lucky," he told him truthfully.

Not bothering to wait for a response, Vicar began to press forward. He stared down at where he penetrated his mate.

Watching himself sink deeper and deeper into Desmond, Vicar felt his brain start to go on the fritz again.

There was just something so damn erotic about watching him sink his cock into his lover, to see himself disappear within the depths of the man he was going to spend the rest of his life with.

When Vicar finally bottomed out, his balls pressed to Desmond's crack, he finally tore his gaze away. He roved his gaze up his mate's lean body, admiring the sweaty gleam on his flushed flesh and the way his abdominals and chest rose and fell with each panting breath. Meeting Desmond's gaze, Vicar reveled in the look of complete bliss that was etched across his features.

Absolutely stunning.

Releasing Desmond's prick, Vicar levered over his mate. He urged him to wrap his leg around his waist before releasing his thigh. Vicar rested his weight on his forearms, bracketing his new and forever lover's head.

"Hello, my mate," Vicar crooned, his heart thudding wildly with the intensity of the moment. Still on his elbows, he reached up and gripped Desmond's hand, threading his fingers with them, before settling both back beside his fox's head. Vicar grinned. "You're mine."

Desmond's answering smile was one of complete rapture, and Vicar planned to see that look often. "Hello, mate," his shifter responded breathlessly. "You're mine, too."

"Yes," Vicar agreed immediately. "Yes, I am."

Holding Desmond's gaze, Vicar began to move. He eased his dick out until he felt his lover's muscles tug at the edges of his crown. For a second, he stilled before he tightened his abdominal muscles and thrust.

Desmond groaned, his head tipping back as his eyelids lowered. His mate bucked under him, telling Vicar he'd nailed it in one. Allowing a feral grin of delight to curve his lips, Vicar did it over and over and over again. He plundered his mate, reveling in the sweet sensations of his mate's chute muscles squeezing and rippling along his cock.

"V-Vic," Desmond whined, doing his best to meet him thrust for thrust. "Oh, gods!"

Lowering his head, Vicar tucked his face against Desmond's neck. "You gonna come for me?" he asked gruffly, never slowing his hips. "You gonna come for your mate?"

"I-I-I—Yes!"

Desmond's cry filled the room. His body arched. His fingers squeezed Vicar's, just as his channel gripped him even tighter.

Vicar snarled, his pleasure cresting, his balls pulling tight. Slamming home one last time, he buried himself as deeply into his mate as he possibly could. He stilled, pouring burst after burst of seed deep inside his forever love.

His senses soaring, Vicar reveled in the knowledge that he was marking his mate internally in the basest of ways. Then the instinct to complete the bond roared through him. Even if Vicar had intended to stop it—which he didn't—he wouldn't have been able to.

Snapping his head forward, Vicar sank his long, sharp canines deep into Desmond's neck. His lover's shout instantly morphed into a throaty moan. As Vicar sucked on the wound, loving the iron-rich flavor of Desmond's life-giving fluid as it flowed across his tastebuds, he felt his lover jolt beneath him once more.

A second later, Vicar felt teeth at his neck. He'd barely registered them before they pierced his skin. The stab of pain was there and gone in a flash to be replaced by a wash of tingling, bliss-inducing pinpricks. They swept down from the bite, across his torso, and felt as if they seeped into his groin. His embedded prick twitched as his testicles forced several more spurts of seed deep inside his lover.

Slowly, after who knew how long, Vicar felt his senses

begin to return to him. He registered Desmond pulling his teeth from him and licking over where he'd bitten. Smiling around Desmond's flesh, he couldn't wait to see the claiming scar his mate had given him. He eased his teeth from Desmond's neck and licked over the wound. Seeing the large scar left behind, a burst of pride flooded Vicar.

"Damn," Vicar muttered huskily, lifting his head to grin at his lover. "My mark looks good on you."

Desmond grinned back at him. "I could say the same to you."

Vicar chuckled as he slid his fingertips through Desmond's pretty auburn hair. "Thank you, Desmond." Enjoying the feel of his mate's hair, even slightly damp from sweat, he told him, "You've made me the happiest damn dragon on earth."

"And I'm the happiest fox shifter," Desmond replied back, gracing Vicar with another of his sweet smiles.

Needing a taste of that, Vicar dipped his head and captured Desmond's mouth. He tasted all the wonderful headiness of before while coupled with the traces of his iron-rich blood. The combination caused a burst of renewed arousal to rush sluggishly through his system.

Vicar began exploring his pretty fox shifter anew.

Yep. Time for round two.

CHAPTER TEN

Slowly rousing, Desmond stretched . . . and immediately let out a soft groan as the muscles of not only his chute but his arms, legs, and abdominals twinged. His well-used body was reminding him of just how voracious — and talented — a lover his dragon was. Over the course of the evening, Desmond had lost count of how many times Vicar had wound him up and sent him soaring.

Just damn! Is this what my life is going to be like now? I'll certainly not complain.

Desmond couldn't help but smile.

"Mmmm, I do like that look on your face." Vicar's voice purred into Desmond's ear as the bed behind him dipped. "What are you thinking about?" Vicar rested a warm hand on his arm, only to slide it under the covers to his hip, squeezing provocatively.

As Desmond opened his eyes, thinking about how to respond, the smell of coffee teased his senses. He turned his head and grinned cheekily at his lover. "I'm grinning about getting served coffee in bed by the sexiest man on earth."

Vicar laughed, the sound a low husky rumble. "Really?" He wrapped his fingers around Desmond's morning semi and squeezed lightly. "Not thinking about this at all?"

A burst of pleasure-pain erupted through Desmond, yanking a moan from his throat. His dick gave a half-hearted twitch even as the muscles of his chute twinged. Groaning again, Desmond gripped Vicar's wrist and squeezed lightly, pulling his hand away.

Upon seeing Vicar's arched brow, Desmond felt his chest warm as a flush heated him from the inside out. "You're insatiable," he whined. "I love it and hate it all at the same time."

Chuckling once more, Vicar eased his wrist from Desmond's grip. "Sorry, baby," he rumbled, his expression turning to understanding. "Just can't seem to get enough of you."

"And I hope that never changes," Desmond assured his dragon, hoping to ease the worried gleam he could see in the big man's black eyes. Waggling his brows, he claimed, "Fortunately, my shifter healing will mean I'll be good to go in no time."

"Until then, how does a nice soak in that big tub I spotted sound?" Vicar offered. He even held out a cup of coffee. "And I couldn't find any creamer, but I can get the milk and sugar if you need it."

Planting his hands on the mattress, Desmond grunted as he sat up. "That's okay." He scooted across the mattress until his back was against the headboard, a pillow between the wood and his skin. "I'm good with black."

Desmond took the offered drink and brought it to his lips. After a tentative sip to test the hotness, he took a much larger swallow. He sighed deeply as he felt the warm liquid slide down his throat.

"Gods, but you are so damn tempting," Vicar growled, then groaned and rested his hands on his jeans-clad legs.

Vicar was wearing a shirt, and Desmond thought that was too bad because the view of his mate's muscles was absolutely delicious.

"So, the tub?" Vicar pressed. Resting a hand on Desmond's upper arm, he caressed Desmond's bicep with his thumb. "Would you like a soak with some bath salts?"

Smirking over the rim of his coffee cup, Desmond asked, "Were you exploring my cupboard?"

Vicar grinned, not appearing at all repentant. "Yep. I most

definitely was." Waggling his dark brows, he claimed, "You can learn a lot about a person by going through their things. And I want to know everything about you."

Recalling that Vicar had asked his friends about him even before the barbeque, Desmond chuckled as he shook his head. "You're incorrigible."

Shrugging his wide shoulders, Vicar continued to grin. "Guilty as charged."

Relaxing with his coffee, Desmond admitted, "I would like a relaxing bath. Thanks." That would help him heal more swiftly. "If you'll join me, anyway."

Vicar growled softly, his eyes narrowing. "If I join you, water may end up all over the floor."

Desmond had guessed that. "We'll put towels down to catch it."

Groaning, Vicar rose to his feet. "After thirty minutes of you in there by yourself, I'll join you," he promised. "You'll need that time to heal."

The way Vicar swept his gaze over Desmond's bare body almost felt like a physical caress, and he felt his body stirring.

Vicar moaned and took a step backward. "Fuck." Pressing the heel of his hand against his groin, he showcased the outline of his erection. "You're just so damn sexy." Vicar pointed toward the bathroom. "You need to soak, and you need food. I'll bring you something."

"You cook?" Desmond asked curiously. While they'd talked a little bit during the night between bouts of love-making, most of the time, they'd just relaxed holding each other, recovering.

"I can get by," Vicar told him. Stepping forward, he dipped and pressed a kiss to Desmond's lips. "Probably not as good as you, though." Straightening, Vicar took a step back once more. "Go relax. I'll be in shortly."

After sweeping a heated gaze over Desmond again, Vicar

whirled and hurried from the room.

Desmond grinned, thinking the man appeared to be fleeing temptation. Chuckling under his breath, he slipped to the edge of the bed. His muscles told him he really did need a break from activity of the calisthenics variety.

Coffee in hand, a smile on his face, Desmond headed to the bathroom.

An hour later, Desmond rested back against Vicar's chest, enjoying the hot water lapping around them. He sighed happily as his dragon stroked lazy circles over his chest and abdominals. It wasn't meant to arouse, but to soothe, and it was working.

Desmond felt his eyelids slide to half-mast. Placing his hands on Vicar's meaty thighs, he settled his head on his strong shoulder. Staring at the bathroom ceiling, Desmond enjoyed the quiet moment.

His stomach was pleasantly full from the biscuits and sausage gravy that Vicar had provided. The dragon had also included hashbrowns and plenty of bacon, both crisped to perfection without being overdone. Along with that, had been more coffee and orange juice.

Desmond hadn't even realized that he had orange juice, but Vicar had assured him that he'd found it in his refrigerator. It had been pushed to the back, but it'd still been within the expiration date. Desmond thought it had been damn nice that the dragon had checked.

He was also relaxed from another fantastic orgasm. While Vicar hadn't fucked him, he had played with his ass with a finger while riding his crease. The slow build had been just as wonderful as the hard fucks of the night before.

"Feeling good, baby?" Vicar murmured, pressing a kiss to Desmond's temple.

"Yeah, thanks." Desmond turned his head and accepted a

deep, languorous kiss. When Vicar lifted his head, Desmond continued to smile at him as he teased, "If that breakfast was *getting by*, I'm a little worried what you think a gourmet meal should be."

Chuckling, Vicar shrugged. "I may have done a little extra." He smiled warmly at him as he admitted, "I didn't want you to think you'd have to do the cooking all the time or we'd starve." After a second of hesitation, Vicar added, "And I liked the idea of taking care of you."

"I liked it, too," Desmond admitted. "I've never had that before."

"Me neither." Vicar pecked a kiss to Desmond's lips again, then just smiled at him. "This is damn nice."

Desmond nodded. "Yeah." Knowing he had to come clean, he murmured, "But that wasn't exactly what I meant."

Vicar cocked his head, his confusion clear. "Are we talking about two different things?"

Snicker-snorting, Desmond nodded. "Afraid so." He squeezed Vicar's thigh. "I meant, I've never had someone interested in taking care of me before. In the past, I'd always have to be the one caring for the other person."

"You've been in relationships before?" Vicar sounded surprised. His smile tightened a little even as his arms clutched him close. "I guess the years can get lonely. Although I didn't think most paranormals did the relationship thing unless they were looking specifically for progeny."

"Yeah, but I wasn't raised in a fox skulk," Desmond admitted.

"No?" Vicar's scent betrayed his shock. "How'd that happen?"

"Well, my mother fell for the sweet words of a player, a human. She thought she was in love," Desmond explained, mentally wincing. "She ended up pregnant. He dropped her, and her skulk kicked her out. We got help from the Shifter

Council, but we didn't join a new skulk or anything. Growing up, I spent a lot more time around humans than I did shifters." Thinking back on those times, Desmond recalled, "There were a couple of guys that I thought were my best friends. When they started dating, I would date, too, so I ended up in and out of a couple of short-term relationships." Meeting Vicar's gaze, Desmond murmured, "Then I met Phil."

Even the hot water couldn't stop Desmond from shivering at the memory of Phil.

Vicar must have felt it, for he rubbed his wet hands over his chest and stomach, then down his thighs and back up to his arms. "You don't have to tell me, if you don't want to, my mate," Vicar murmured into his ear. "I won't let anyone harm you again, and I won't harm you the way that asshole must have."

Relaxing under his ministrations, Desmond sighed deeply. That offer was damn tempting. Except, he needed Vicar to know, especially if he slipped up and flinched or something. Desmond never wanted to hurt his mate, but he still had a few ingrained habits that he needed to explain.

"I need to tell you," Desmond whispered. He turned a little in Vicar's arms, so he could more easily look up at him while still being in his embrace. "I still flinch. You saw that at the cafeteria." Desmond hated when he did it, but sometimes, he couldn't help himself. "If I do it when you reach for me, I want you to know that it's not you. It's still something I'm working on. I'll get there."

Vicar nodded slowly. "Okay." His deep voice remained soft, and his hands gently massaged Desmond's body. "So, I take it Phil was abusive."

Nibbling his bottom lip, Desmond nodded. "Yeah. He was human. Big, although not as big as you." He smiled weakly as he peered at Vicar through his lashes. "Guess I always had a weakness for big men, and Fate sure gave me my dream come true."

Smiling, Vicar dipped his head and pressed a chaste kiss to Desmond's lips. "Thank you, my mate." Tracing a wet finger along Desmond's jawline, he told him, "I think she chose perfectly for me, too."

Desmond warmed at the praise, the sensation beating out the chill that thinking about Phil had caused. "Okay, so." He hesitated, wondering where to begin. "Um, he was really nice in the beginning. When he asked me to move in with him, I was tempted. I told Phil I needed to think about it. The next day, Phil presented me with travel plans. He'd rented a cabin for five days. He said it would be a great trial run, as well as a kickass vacation." Desmond forced himself to keep talking, even though he still felt like a fool for accepting the invitation. "It was remote. There were hiking trails and such, and he knew I loved the outdoors." Meeting Vicar's gaze, he told him, "The second day there, he grabbed me by the hair. I wore it longer back then. He yanked my head back and stared down at me with this look of disgust and loathing in his eyes. He told me he knew I was a monster. I still don't know how Phil knew I was a shifter, but he forced me into a cage. I was in there for three days unless he decided to pull me out and beat me. I shifted and tried to attack him, to get away, but he was so damn strong." Shaking his head, Desmond scowled at the side of the tub, appreciating Vicar's silence so he could get it all out. "He would grab me by the scruff and shake me until I shifted back. Then he'd use my hair to control me."

Desmond paused, losing himself in the memories for a moment.

Vicar gently teased along his jaw, urging him to lift his gaze and focus on him. "So, when people reach for your face or hair, you shy away," he murmured, his expression full of understanding. "I do love the feel of your hair. I won't lie." Smiling just a little, Vicar added, "But I'll be careful. I'll always make certain you know my touch is coming."

As Vicar spoke, he eased his fingers up the side of Desmond's face toward his hair. He skimmed his fingers between the strands. His nails scratched lightly, offering a massage of sorts.

Sighing, Desmond tipped his head into Vicar's touch. It truly felt fantastic. Tingles spread across his head, down his neck, and across his chest. Even his nipples beaded.

"Now, that's a wonderful look on you," Vicar rumbled, dipping his head to lap at his lips before sealing his mouth over Desmond's. For a moment, Vicar lapped and teased sensuously, as if making love to his mouth. Finally, Vicar broke the kiss and smiled down at him. "Yeah, definitely a good look."

"Love your kisses," Desmond admitted. Lifting a hand, he teased his fingertip around Vicar's full black lips. "So sexy."

Vicar continued to hold Desmond's gaze as he turned his head and sucked that finger into his mouth. He nipped the pad lightly before releasing it.

"All yours, baby," Vicar rumbled with a heated smile. The look slipped away swiftly enough, and he asked, "Is Phil the man Priest saved you from?"

Desmond nodded, recalling the big black lion shifter that had stumbled upon them. "He was on assignment hunting a rogue in the area." Scoffing softly, he murmured, "I still remember this big, black stranger bursting through the door. I was in the cage, and at first, he scared me to death." Desmond didn't dwell on the memory too often. It was bloody. "Suffice it to say, Priest killed Phil without saying a word to the guy. I thought he was an ax murderer or something, and I would be next," he admitted with a scoff. "But then Priest crouched in front of the cage and stated, *You're safe now, little shifter. Let's get you home.* Then he opened the cage, helped me out, and took me to the council. They prepared new identities for myself and my mom. I got a job in their cafeteria, and I've been there ever since."

Nodding slowly, Vicar eyed him sagely. "You had a crush on Priest," he commented astutely.

Unable to help himself, Desmond blushed as he let out a groan. "Yeah. Hero worship and all." Resting his palms on Vicar's chest, he met his gaze and assured, "But I got over that a long time ago, and we never did anything together." Snorting, Desmond added, "I'm so not Priest's type."

"How is that possible?" Vicar appeared offended on Desmond's behalf. "You're perfect. You're everyone's type."

Snickering, Desmond shook his head. "Naw, but thanks. Priest likes twinks. Blond and pale. The paler, the better." With a shrug, he added, "Maybe it's the whole opposites attract thing."

Desmond beamed up at Vicar as he eased onto his knees. Swinging his leg over his mate's thigh, he made himself comfortable on the big dragon's lap. He slid his hands up Vicar's neck and up even more, enjoying the feel of his smooth scalp.

"Anyway, thank you for listening to me," Desmond murmured, liking how Vicar immediately settled his hands on his hips, holding him close. "I appreciate you letting me explain."

"I'll do my best to always listen to you," Vicar told him, his smile warm. As he rubbed one hand up and down Desmond's side, he narrowed his eyes and rumbled, "So what would you like to talk about now?"

"Talking's overrated," Desmond whispered before stretching up and capturing Vicar's mouth.

To Desmond's pleasure, Vicar didn't hesitate to return the kiss.

CHAPTER ELEVEN

Vicar stared at the small craftsman-style home and felt an odd surge of nerves.

How could the idea of meeting one small woman cause him such trepidation? Except, it did. This was Desmond's mother. He'd known his mate and his mother were a package deal from the start.

What if she doesn't like me? Or approve of me?

"Are you okay?"

Yanking his gaze to Desmond, Vicar saw him already standing outside. He still had the door open, and he peered in at him. Concern filled his expression and began permeating into the *Jeep*.

"Uh, is it odd to be . . . worried?" Vicar asked slowly, deciding to confide in his mate. They were a team, after all. "If she doesn't like me, will she try to cause problems between us?"

Desmond smiled reassuringly. "Mom'll love you." He winked and gave him a cheesy eyebrow waggle. "Just not the way I love you."

Vicar sighed deeply as he pushed his door open. "I'm being serious, Desmond." He closed the door before moving to meet his mate near the hood. Resting his hands on Desmond's hips, Vicar pinned him with a serious look. "You're her baby. Hell, without a skulk, she's your reason for living. What if she's not happy about . . . us?"

Resting his hands on Vicar's chest, Desmond rubbed soothingly. "My mom really will be happy for us," he told him.

"She'll be absolutely ecstatic that I've found my fated mate." With a small shrug, Desmond added, "She may even be a little jealous, but she'll deal with it."

Needing to trust his mate, Vicar nodded. "Okay. Let's do this then." After those words, he turned and slid his right arm around Desmond's waist.

To Vicar's pleasure, Desmond mirrored the move. He even tucked his fingers into Vicar's belt loop near his hip. Together, they started up the short walk to the front door.

Even before they reached the small front porch, Vicar saw the door open. A petite woman with auburn hair that had a bit more blonde in it than her son's appeared on the porch, but her eyes were the same warm brown as Desmond's. She glanced between them, obviously taking in the way Desmond and Vicar held each other.

So, this is Marisa Takara.

"I thought that sounded like your *Jeep*, Des," she greeted, although she appeared a little worried. "You usually work on Thursdays. Is everything okay?"

"Everything's fine, Mom," Desmond assured as they took the couple of steps to stop on the porch. "More than fine, actually." Grinning broadly, Desmond indicated Vicar. "I'd like to introduce you to Vicar Rhomes." He paused for a heartbeat, perhaps for dramatic effect. "Vicar is my mate." Lowering his voice, Desmond added, "My fated mate."

The woman froze for a few seconds before her jaw sagged open. "Your fated mate?" she whispered, clearly disbelieving. "Truly? You're sure?"

"Yes," Desmond replied firmly. "I'm certain."

Then Marisa squealed even as she danced in place. A second later, she threw her arms around both of them and squeezed them tightly. Before Vicar could decide if he should return the embrace, Marisa released them and rushed to the door.

"Come in, come in," Marisa urged, yanking the door open

with such force that the hinges creaked. She giggled as she beckoned with her other hand. "I want to hear all about you, Vicar. How did you meet? What do you do?"

Due to Desmond's urging, Vicar started forward. As they passed by her, Marisa gave a none-too-discreet sniff.

"And I'm a little curious as to what you are, too," Marisa stated, closing the door behind them. "I don't recognize your scent."

"Not surprising, really," Vicar replied. His smile came easily, relief having flooded him upon seeing her exuberance. "I'm a dragon."

Marisa gaped. Then her legs seemed to fall out from under her, and she plopped onto the boot box situated near the door. Peering up at him, she just continued to stare.

Extricating himself, Desmond hurried to his mother's side. "Mom?" He knelt on one knee next to her and took one of her hands between both of his own. "Momma? Are you okay?"

After a couple of blinks, Marisa tore her attention away from Vicar to focus on Desmond. "A dragon?" she whispered, clearly disbelieving.

Desmond nodded, his smile encouraging. "Yeah, Momma." He glanced up at Vicar with warmth in his eyes before refocusing on Marisa. "Vicar's a dragon."

"They exist?"

Yup. She's having a hard time believing.

"We exist," Vicar assured, standing uncertainly. He wasn't entirely sure what to do with himself. "We stay hidden, just like other paranormals."

"Wow." Marisa blinked a few more times. Then she lifted her attention to him, a wan smile curving her features. "Sorry. Just—" Marisa barked a short laugh. "Boy howdy." She used her free hand to pat one of Desmond's. "Way to try to give your momma a heart attack, baby boy."

Desmond chuckled as he shook his head. "Sorry, Momma." Shrugging, he told her, "Guess I don't think I told you about my buddy, Charon, huh?"

"The human who works in the kitchens with you?" Marisa cocked her head, confusion filling her scent. "What's he have to do with it?"

"We have a few things to explain," Desmond revealed, shaking his head. Rising to his feet, he helped his mother to stand. "Let's make some coffee, Momma." Wrapping his arm around Marisa's waist, he began guiding her deeper into the house. "Any chance you made any snickerdoodles recently?"

"Of course, sweetie," Marisa replied with a smile. "I'll get the cookies. You make the coffee." She peered up at Vicar. "Do you like snickerdoodles, son?"

Vicar almost laughed. He couldn't remember anyone calling him son in . . . a very long time. Still, he resisted and answered her. "I'm not certain, ma'am," Vicar told her. "I can't recall trying a cookie called snickerdoodles."

"What a shame," Marisa cried, clearly shocked. "Well, don't you worry none, sweetie. I'm sure you'll like these." Without missing a beat, she added, "And call me Momma or Marisa." Reaching for his hand as she passed him, Marisa squeezed his hand. "You're family, after all."

Never in Vicar's wildest dreams would he have imagined someone asking him to call her Momma. In truth, he didn't know if he would be able to. Still, he could fulfill her second option.

"Thank you, Marisa."

The pretty woman beamed up at him, then hustled into the kitchen.

Vicar followed slowly, wondering how his life was well and truly changing.

They're good changes, though.

"Oh, my." Marisa stared at Vicar with wide eyes. "You dumped chowder on my poor boy?"

"Afraid so," Vicar confirmed with a wince. "My attention

was on my king, and I didn't look where I was going."

"And my senses were confused by the spicy jambalaya I was carrying, so I didn't realize it, either," Desmond cut in with a laugh. Sitting next to Vicar on the small sofa, he squeezed Vicar's thigh lightly. "Then I took off my shirt and—"

"And it was like being hit by a two-by-four, but in a good way," Vicar explained, relieved that Desmond had decided to skip over the part about Vicar yelling at him. "We scheduled to meet up at Delanrue's barbeque last night, and we've been getting to know each other ever since." Pinning Desmond with an appreciative look, Vicar grabbed his hand and brought it to his lips for a kiss. "And I couldn't be happier."

"Oh, my." Marisa's voice sounded as if she were fighting back tears, and when Vicar returned his focus to her, he noticed the way her eyes gleamed. "That's so wonderful." Marisa rested her hands on her breasts. "So that's why you're not working today. How long do you have off to forge your bond?" Leaning forward, she asked, "Have you bitten each other, yet?"

Desmond groaned, his cheeks taking on a pinkish hue. "Momma," he said on a whine.

Vicar swallowed his chuckle. After all, he had no desire to discuss their sex life with Marisa, either. "Yes, that's why Desmond has the day off."

Vicar had overheard Head Enforcer Mycroft when he'd called Desmond that morning. The cheetah shifter had congratulated him, then told him to take a couple of weeks to get to know his mate before letting him know if he would be returning. When Desmond had questioned his boss, Mycroft had gently reminded him that Vicar lived in another state.

At the time, Vicar had mentally winced. Fortunately, his shifter hadn't denied him right that second. He'd made a comment about forgetting about that. Then Desmond had thanked Mycroft and hung up the phone.

"Wait, did you say you were watching your king?" Marisa's voice cut into Vicar's thoughts, drawing him back into the conversation. "The dragons are ruled by a king?" Then she tittered as she swept her gaze over him. "Makes sense. You look very formidable." Marisa winked at Vicar before focusing on Desmond and winking. "Fate sure did treat you right."

Desmond opened his mouth, then snapped it shut again, as if he had no idea how to respond to that.

Vicar didn't either. He was about to reach for his cup of coffee when his phone buzzed at his hip.

Damn. Saved by the bell.

Reaching down, Vicar pulled his phone free. His brows shot up. "Speak of the devil," he murmured. After squeezing Desmond's hand, he released him and rose to his feet. "I'm sorry. I need to take this."

"Sure." Desmond smiled at him before refocusing on his mother. "Yeah, uh. Dragons are ruled by a king, and his name is Leortis." Clearing his throat, he chuckled depreciatively. "I've met him. He's a really nice guy. Mated to a human."

"Hello, sire," Vicar greeted, moving toward the dining room. "What can I help you with?"

"I'm sorry to interrupt you when you're bonding with your new mate," Leortis responded in lieu of a greeting. "I'd planned to give you a couple of days, but something's come up."

"It always does, doesn't it?" Vicar replied with a sigh. Rubbing over his bald scalp, he couldn't help but recall how Leortis had been called in to fight for his position as king the same evening he'd met his own mate. *Shit happens.* "I understand duty. You know that."

"I know how important doing your duty is, old friend." Leortis lowered his voice. "We have a lead on Gaithnos. I need you to meet me at Shifter Headquarters as soon as possible."

"Huh, I'm not entirely certain how long I'll be," Vicar admitted, scowling. "We're at Desmond's mother's house. I'll need to get an *Uber* or something to take me back to the hotel so I can pick up a vehicle."

"You can use my *Jeep*," Desmond offered, appearing at his side. Touching his right upper arm, his mate held out his keys in the other. "I need to stay here and explain moving to my mom."

Even as Vicar took the keys, he asked, "Are you certain?"

"Take him up on the offer, Vicar," Leortis ordered through the line. "The faster you get here, the faster you can return to him."

Desmond smirked. "Call me when you're on your way back."

Vicar nodded once. "I will." Then he dipped his head and pressed a hard kiss to Desmond's lips. "I hope it'll be quick." After Desmond nodded, Vicar started back through the house. He waved at Marisa as he started toward the front door. "It was nice meeting you, ma'am." Vicar winced before amending, "Marisa. I'm sure I'll see you again soon."

Marisa nodded, rising to her feet. "Yes, we will." Pointing at him, she added, "Stay safe, son."

Yup. That still sounds weird.

"Yes, m—Marisa."

Damn, that'll take some getting used to, too.

As Vicar hurried out the door, he brought his phone back to his ear. "Can you tell me anything?" he asked as he pulled the driver's door open.

"I'll tell you when you get here," Leortis stated. Then he sounded amused while saying, "I'd tell you to hurry, but getting caught speeding would only slow you down."

Then his king disconnected the line.

Rolling his eyes, Vicar climbed behind the wheel and

placed his cell into a cup holder. Before even starting the *Jeep*, he had to move the seat back. Thinking of his much shorter mate, Vicar smiled and started on his way.

A little over twenty minutes later, Vicar turned the *Jeep* into the driveway for the golf course and spa that covered as the Shifter Headquarters. He drove around to the underground parking and found a spot. Then Vicar paused, wondering where to go.

Fortunately, someone must have been watching for him. Enforcer Germaine—a tall, slender anaconda shifter—opened a door to the left and waved to get his attention. Once Vicar was focused on the enforcer, he beckoned.

Vicar strode toward Germaine swiftly. "You my escort?" he asked.

Germaine grinned. "Yep." Tipping his head to the side, he urged, "Come on. I'll show you where King Leortis is holed up with a few others."

Scenting the honesty in the man's words, Vicar fell into step beside him. "You know anything about what's going on?"

"Afraid not," Germaine admitted. "One of our tech guys, Link, got an alert. He notified Councilman Goldstein, who passed the information on to your king." Tapping the phone at his belt, Germaine finished, "Councilman Goldstein just texted me to meet you."

Vicar nodded and fell silent. After all, there wasn't anything else to say.

As Vicar walked into the room Germaine indicated, he automatically checked out the occupants. Royal Guard Warzer stood behind where King Leortis sat with Kitoman flanking him on the other side. Councilman Goldstein was in the room as well as another couple of shifters he didn't recognize. The one near the councilman was obviously an enforcer. While the man in front of the vast array of computers probably could have been an enforcer, judging by his size, his fingers flew over the keyboard, making Vicar think he must be Link.

"Thank you for getting here so swiftly," King Leortis stated, looking over at him. "Sorry to drag you away from your new mate." After a sniff, Leortis winced. "Your newly bonded mate."

"He understands," Vicar assured his king. "He—" Hearing his phone ring, he paused and pulled it out. Frowning, Vicar murmured, "Desmond's calling."

"Better take it," Leortis encouraged. "I know you're all about duty, but if he's calling you right after lending you his *Jeep*, it must be important."

Nodding, Vicar took Leortis's advice. He took the call and lifted his phone to his ear. "Desmond? What's wrong?" he asked, not bothering with a greeting.

"You have something I want, Vicar." A deep rumbly voice came through the line. A cold smugness filled the tone. "And I have something you want."

Vicar felt his heart constrict in his chest. He recognized the speaker's voice.

"What do you want, Gaithnos?" Vicar snarled, worry and fear gnawing at him. He noticed everyone who'd been seated began to stand, save for Link. "Where's Desmond?"

Fuck! I just left him! How could Gaithnos have him?

"Drop Charon's welp off at a location I designate, and I'll return your mate."

Vicar felt his gut clench as he stared around the room. He knew that every paranormal in the room had heard Gaithnos's demand. Link spun in his chair and made a *keep him talking* motion.

Even as bile threatened to come up his throat just at the idea of handing over Charon and Dakota's babe to the psycho dragon, Vicar asked, "And how the fuck do expect me to do that?"

And it's so not happening. There's gotta be another way.

CHAPTER TWELVE

Hearing the deep guttural voice pulled Desmond out of his sleep. The pounding in his head registered.

Nope. Not sleep. I was knocked out.

Desmond did his best to keep his breathing even, slow and even, as he fought back flashbacks of his past.

I'm not in a cage. I'm not being held by Phil.

Then the stranger's words registered. "Drop Charon's welp off at a location I designate, and I'll return your mate."

Oh shit. What the hell?

Just that fast, what happened came rushing back.

As soon as Vicar left, his mother jumped from her seat, grabbed his hands, and asked, "Are you happy?"

"Yeah," Desmond claimed, smiling at her. "Most definitely happy."

His mother sighed, giving him a fond look. "I'll miss you, baby boy."

"No, you won't," Desmond denied, shaking his head. Before she could counter him, he told her, "Because Vicar is a good man who knows we're a package deal. When he comes back, he has every intention of asking you to move with us."

Gasping, his mother stared at him with wide eyes. "Me live with dragons?" When Desmond nodded in confirmation, she squeaked, "Live with the dragon king?"

Smirking, Desmond teased, "Well, I'm pretty sure the king and his mate have their own wing, but . . . yeah, in the same building or close to it."

"Oh my goodness." His mother released him and sat back on the sofa. When she shook her head, Desmond began to worry that she was going to refuse. "Me with dragons. Never would have thought of that." Then she bounced right back to her feet and beamed at him. "Well, I better go get some boxes. I'll head to the grocery store and see what they have in the back." After pecking a kiss to Desmond's cheek, she squeezed him one more time before hustling from the house, all the while mumbling about moving in with dragons.

Less than a moment later, Desmond heard his mother's little hatchback fire up, heralding her leaving.

Desmond stood in the living room, amusement and worry filling him, and he hoped she remembered to curtail her tongue before reaching the store.

Just when Desmond decided to cook a meal, since it seemed they would be busy spending the afternoon sorting and packing, he heard the sound of breaking glass. He whipped around, barely managing to register the hulking older man before pain slammed through his temple.

Then it was lights out.

"I know you're awake," his kidnapper stated. A low growl entered the deep voice as he demanded, "Look at me when I speak to you."

At least my mother is safe. She wasn't there.

Slowly, carefully, Desmond blinked open his eyes. It took him a couple of tries to focus. When he managed it, he found himself surprised by the surroundings. While the drapes to all the nearby windows had been pulled mostly shut, Desmond had no trouble making things out.

Desmond lay on a leather sofa in what appeared to be the living or central room of what looked to be a lodge or large cabin-like building. There was a massive, two-story fireplace in the corner. The chimney was all colorful river rock, and the hearth appeared to be slate. A huge elk head hung high overhead upon it.

Several more leather sofas and chairs dotted the area around him. There was a coffee table before him, and a good-sized TV hung on the wall off to his left.

Slowly, Desmond sat up. He panned his gaze to the right and spotted a log staircase leading to the second level. Standing in the shadows on the loft level above, Desmond made out a figure so imposing he couldn't help but suck in a sharp breath.

"Who are you?"

Desmond felt damn pleased that he managed to keep his voice steady.

"I'm Elder Gaithnos."

Gaithnos. Shit. The rogue dragon.

This is so much worse than Phil.

Recalling the order Gaithnos had given . . . someone . . . Desmond shoved those thoughts from his mind. They had no place in his brain if he were to keep his wits about him. He knew that, dealing with a dragon, he would definitely need his wits.

"Why do you want Charon and Dakota's son?" Desmond asked, hoping for more information. In his experience, information meant a greater chance at escape. "Are you going to raise him as your own?"

Gaithnos scoffed as he slowly moved toward the stairs. "Please. Me? An elder dragon raising an omega?" The afternoon light from a second-story window flashed across Gaithnos just right as he moved, betraying his cold sneer. "Of course not. I need money."

"Money?" Confusion filled Desmond, and his gut curdled just a little. "Are you going to ransom him back to Charon and Dakota?"

Barking a laugh, Gaithnos shook his head. He paused in a

sunbeam about halfway down the stairs and stared imperiously at him, his expression haughty. "Those two reprobates could never gather the amount of money that I need to stay ahead of the king's men." Leaning a hip on the thick wooden railing, he smirked. "Oh, no. Charon ruined my life, so I'm going to take his welp and sell it to a dragon weir that likes to raise omegas as breeders. There's still a few of them out there, and they'll pay a pretty penny for the half-breed."

Gasping, Desmond leaped to his feet. "You're going to sell him for *breeding*?" he cried, absolutely stricken.

"Of course." Gaithnos didn't sound the least bit upset at the prospect. In fact, he sounded eager as a low rumble filled his voice. "I love the idea of Charon knowing his welp is out there somewhere, being a breeder, and he can do nothing to stop it."

"So you know what those other dragons are doing is wrong, right? That treating an omega as nothing but a vessel to pop out more babies is . . . *wrong*." Desmond's mind fritzed as he racked his brain for a better explanation. "Vile. Despicable. Evil!"

"Charon cost me my son!" Gaithnos roared, his voice taking on a pitch that told him the man's dragon was damn close to the surface. With a growling yell, he continued, "I will make Charon pay a thousand times over for that!"

Gaithnos roared so loudly that the house shook around them.

Desmond staggered backward. Even as he flailed his arms, he stumbled, unable to catch himself. Landing on his ass with a thump, Desmond hissed, his head bumping against the side of the coffee table leg. Desmond resisted the urge to shake his head, knowing that would probably exacerbate the ache there.

Instead, Desmond turned over and curled up on his side. While he never took his attention off of the dragon on the steps — the man had his head tipped back and was laughing at him as if seeing him fall over was the funniest fucking thing ever — something caught his attention to the right. From the corner of his eye, Desmond processed what he saw.

On the other side of the sofa was the dining room. Beyond that, he saw a huge bar with seating for six, denoting the start of the kitchen. To the right of the refrigerator was a door — a door with a doggie door.

Can I get outside? What are the chances it's locked?

Desmond stilled, his body seizing as he contemplated taking the chance.

Oh, who gives a fuck. I gotta try. After all, he needs me alive . . . right?

While pushing away the fact that being needed alive didn't mean he was needed hale and healthy, Desmond rolled to his knees. He whined a little, making himself sound piteous. Then he began to crawl around the edge of the sofa.

"Where the fuck do you think you're going?" Even as Gaithnos cussed at him, his question came out modulated, as if he thought the answer was beneath him.

"W-Water," Desmond murmured. Recalling his time with Phil and how the asshole had loved hearing him beg for the simplest of things, he added a little whimper to his voice while begging, "Please."

Gods, begging this asshole sucks.

All the while, Desmond continued to crawl toward the kitchen. He noticed the door wasn't particularly large, maybe with a medium-sized dog in mind. Fortunately, even though he was a shifter, Desmond knew he was still a small fox.

Maybe it was because of his human father.

"Very well." Gaithnos waved his hand imperiously, as if he were granting a great wish. "Get some water."

Desmond moved into the kitchen. The sink was in the island, so once he was behind it, he rose to his knees and turned on the faucet. Using the noise of the faucet to hide the tell-tale snap of bone and pop of muscle moving beneath his skin, Desmond reached for his fox and shifted.

In his fox form, Desmond wasn't a whole lot bigger than his human frame. Except his legs were shorter. Fortunately, his waist was trimmer, too, so while he couldn't do anything about the red shirt he wore, Desmond easily shimmied out of his jeans. Sitting on his rump, he grabbed first one sock in his teeth and yanked it off, then the second.

"Hey, what are you doing?" Gaithnos's heavy gait thudded down the stairs. Lethal warning dripping from his tone, he snarled, "Don't make me chase you."

Ignoring him, Desmond jumped to his paws and bolted toward the doggie door. He lowered his head and cocked it to the side. Even as he lunged for the plastic flap, Desmond led with his shoulder.

Desmond felt the tip of his nose knock against the side of the small rectangular opening, but the flap easily gave way. In the next instant, his paws hit the wooden slats of a back deck . . . and nearly went right out from under him. Digging in his claws, Desmond caught himself.

Seeing the thick tree trunks all around, Desmond realized he had to be at least two stories up. He spotted the stairs, but they were behind a gate. Running toward it, he gauged the distance to the landing on the other side and leaped. When he landed, Desmond once again slid, and his shoulder slammed into the railing.

With a quick jump to his paws, Desmond started down the stairs. As he ran, he heard an almighty roar. The house shook as glass and wood shards suddenly sprayed all around him. The pieces raining down on his back didn't bother him, but then Desmond stepped on a piece of glass, causing him to yelp as it bit deep.

On three legs, Desmond made it to the bottom of the stairs. He paused long enough to inspect his paw, and he spotted the bit of glass sticking out of it. More than happy to be a shifter with a brain that could analyze, Desmond carefully used his teeth to pull it out.

"I smell you, little shifter," Gaithnos declared, his voice deep and rumbly in dragon form. "Come back, or you'll pay for wasting my time and energy."

Desmond ignored him.

Knowing a posh place such as this had to be connected to a road system, Desmond started running. Unfortunately, the deck had overlooked a ravine. When he tried to round the house, he faced a tall rock retaining wall.

Instead of trying to scale it, Desmond raced into the deep undergrowth . . . and immediately found himself tumbling ass over teakettle down a steep incline. When his back hit a tree, stopping his descent, he couldn't help the yelp that escaped. The whoosh of wind overhead caused him to jerk his focus upward, and a chill swept down his spine.

Hovering nearly fifty feet above him, only kept at bay by the trees, was a massive red dragon.

As Desmond watched, the dragon opened his jaws and inhaled deeply. A glow of red appeared between his teeth.

Desmond jumped to his paws and braved the ravine even as he felt the heat of the fire and the occasional singe of sparks. He fell more than ran as he made his way down the sidestep incline. To his surprise, Desmond found himself tumbling out from beneath some underbrush and into a decent-sized clearing. Within it ran a stream.

As Desmond found his paws and began galloping toward it, he noticed a set of stairs to his right. If he had to guess, they were the path a human would take.

Oh well.

The wind kicked up around him again, signaling Gaithnos's approach.

Shit!

Turning toward the stream, Desmond gauged the strength

of the moving water.

How fast will it carry me downstream?

Before Desmond had a chance to decide, a loud roar carried through the air. Something thudded loudly overhead. A second later, he had to skitter out of the way as two huge forms crashed into the earth, nearly right on top of him.

Desmond streaked into the forest as fire erupted, followed by icy tendrils, dousing them. Turning to watch, he crept forward. While he didn't consider himself brave, Desmond knew several things to be true.

First off, any dragon attacking Gaithnos had to be against him, so maybe he could use his help. Especially if the guy was a guard or enforcer or something. Second of all, Desmond wouldn't know which way to run to avoid getting squashed by their huge bodies or flames if he didn't keep an eye on them. The third and final thing was, if this guy took Gaithnos out, Desmond could easily get out of the woods and hunt down his mate.

Peering between leaves, Desmond did his best to keep quiet as he took in the spectacle before him. A mammoth black dragon clamped his massive jaws around Gaithnos's neck, sinking his teeth deep between scales and drawing blood. With a twist of his body, he easily avoided the club on the end of Gaithnos's tail. Using that momentum, the black dragon slammed his spiked tail into Gaithnos's underbelly, drawing a roar of pain from the other beast.

As Desmond watched Gaithnos arch his neck with pain, he would have felt bad for the guy . . . if it weren't for what he knew the bastard intended to do to his friends' son.

"Vicar!" a deep voice called from above. "That's enough. I want him alive."

A second later, a dark blue dragon Desmond recognized as King Leortis settled into the small clearing beside the struggling pair. "Submit, Gaithnos. Or you won't leave here alive."

Gaithnos roared as he turned his neck and blew a stream

of fire toward Leortis. The king lifted out of range before closing the distance. Using his spiked tail like a club, Leortis whomped the other dragon on his head.

With a groan, Gaithnos dropped, and the red dragon lay still.

"Release him, Vicar," Leortis ordered again.

After doing just that, although he never took his attention away from the downed dragon, the black dragon rumbled, "Damn it, Leortis. How am I supposed to find my mate now?"

It suddenly hit Desmond. That huge, fierce black dragon was his mate.

Excitement building within him, Desmond yipped and jumped from where he hid. He bounced into the clearing, his bushy red tail wagging as if he were a dog—not that he would ever admit that to another. When both dragons focused on him, Desmond figured he should have been concerned, but he wasn't.

Leortis's deep blue lips actually curved into a dragon smile. "Ah, there's your mate now." The king thumped Vicar with a wing. "Warzer and I will take care of this asshole. You take care of your mate."

"Desmond?" Vicar rumbled, lowering his head to peer at him with one large, black eye. "Are you okay?" His huge nostrils widened before he growled, "I smell blood."

Knowing he couldn't answer as a fox, Desmond quickly shifted. Amusement filled him when Vicar used a great black wing to hide his nudity from the king, as well as a large green dragon landing beside them—Warzer, apparently.

Desmond gripped the top edge of his mate's wing and grinned up at Vicar. "I knew you'd come, but how'd you find me so quickly?"

"I smell blood," Vicar growled, ignoring his question.

With a roll of his eyes, Desmond held up his palm. "Just got cut on some glass from when asshole here decided to bust out the wall of the house." That was what he assumed had happened, anyway. "I really am good." Desmond used his other hand to rub over Vicar's wing, which he thought felt really cool. "And you should totally question that asshole." Glaring at the downed Gaithnos, Desmond told them, "He said he was going to sell Charon and Dakota's son to a dragon weir that likes to use omegas for breeding. That's a dragon group, right? Like a fox skulk?" After getting a nod from Vicar, Desmond growled and returned his glare to the unconscious red dragon. "How sick is that? We need to find those assholes and shut 'em down."

Leortis growled deeply. "I'll get that information extracted from him," the king assured. "Don't you worry, little fox."

Jerking a nod, Desmond grumbled, "Good." Then he peered up at his mate. Even as he admired Vicar's stunning dragon form, he asked, "So, uh, how did you find me so fast?"

Vicar scoffed deeply. "The moron used your phone to call me. Your people tracked it."

Desmond couldn't help but bark a laugh. "Wow. Total rookie move."

"Yes." Then Vicar lowered his head and gently nuzzled the tip of his snout against Desmond's cheek. "You're a very pretty fox," he somehow managed to purr. "And we never did get to play chase. This is a perfect area." Then Vicar's dragon voice even managed to deepen. "And to the winner goes the spoils."

Sucking in a sharp gasp, Desmond felt his body flush with the need to reconnect with his mate. He'd been in danger, and his lover had been in a fight. His nature demanded that they reconnect.

With a groan, Desmond muttered, "Yes, please."

"Don't worry," Leortis drawled. "I'll let your mother know you're fine."

Oops!

Beaming at the king, Desmond called, "Thanks so much!"

Desmond didn't wait for an answer. Although he did hear the rumbling sounds of dragon chuckles, his need was riding him too hard. He shifted. Less than a moment later, he'd returned to fox form, and he peered up at his dragon expectantly.

Vicar lowered his massive snout and nuzzled him. Then he gripped the tattered remains of the shirt that still clung to him. With a jerk, Vicar tore it from his body.

With a yipping laugh, Desmond turned and sprinted into the brush.

Desmond felt the wind pick up around him, and adrenaline thrummed through him for a whole new reason.

Time to play chase with my mate.

As Desmond ducked, bobbed, jumped, and weaved through the brush and trees, he knew this wouldn't be the only time they would do this together.

My life with my amazing mate is right on track.

ABOUT THE AUTHOR

Charlie started writing fantasy when she was eight, and after stumbling onto her first erotic romance at age nineteen, she realized her true calling. She now focuses on writing gay erotic romance, normally of the paranormal variety, with heroes of all kinds. With the help and support of her husband, Charlie finally fulfilled one of her life-long goals . . . move to acreage with her horses. You can often find her curled up with her laptop and a cup of tea or glass of wine, creating her next adventure. Charlie enjoys exploring the mountains of her new Oregon home on horseback, 4-wheeler, or motorcycle.

She can be reached at ch.richards2010@yahoo.com

Or visit her at www.charlie-richards.com.

www.ingramcontent.com/pod-product-compliance
Lightning Source LLC
Chambersburg PA
CBHW070455130626
46555CB00003B/1014